LET'S GIT U
THE TA.

A social history of diet and cooking in the Essex and East Anglian region largely from the words of those who did the growing, the cooking and the eating.

by Basil Slaughter

Illustrated by
Grace Bevan (Writtle WEA)

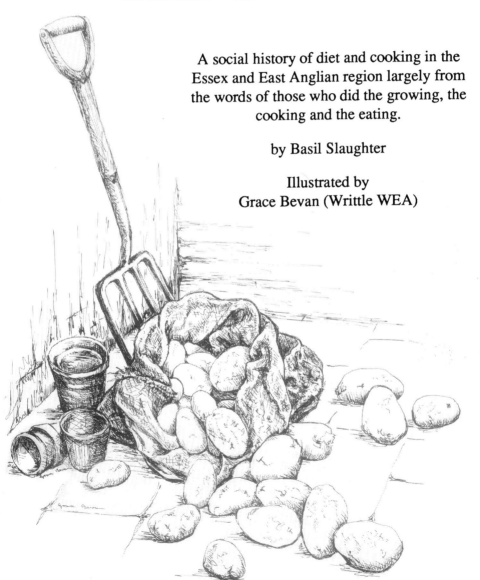

AUTHOR'S NOTE

This book is dedicated to all those people who helped write it by giving me interviews, allowing tape recordings in their homes and contributing to discussion during my talks.

Now read some things that down in these ould parts
Lie nearest to their stummicks or their hearts
Do you take heed o' them, they done their best
To put the story through – and for the rest
If you do find it hard this howdeyedo to weather
Jest blaime the duzzy fule whas put this lot together.
(With apologies to S. L. Bensusan)

Suffolk in the early 19th century used the word SAY (or sah) to describe a taste of or first try at something (essay?). South Essex said "I'll just take a twothry" when it wished to sample a dish. At least Gepp spells it thus but I wonder if it could be "toothry".

A PINGLER in both counties was a person who had no stomach for a proper meal but picked a bit, with no appetite. The book, arranged as a dictionary, is designed for both users, pinglers and proper readers, dippers and devourers so to sit down to a meal is to "Git up agin the Table".

© Copyright Hilary Slaughter 1992   © Copyright Illustrations Grace Bevan 1992

ISBN 0 9519265 0 0

Published by the Essex Federation of the Workers Educational Association, 172 Lexden Road, Colchester.

Printed by Beeleigh Litho, Witham

Basil Slaughter lived a very busy and creative life, as a husband and father, a teacher, the headmaster of a village school and a leading member of Essex WEA, and so had little time in which to record more than a few samples of his remarkable understanding of the rural past of Essex and Suffolk.

His "Essex and Suffolk Alphabet", an hilarious composition, and his "Bulmer, Then and Now", a model history of his own village, are almost all that we have to commemorate his contribution to our region's local history, except for the memory of the stories, impressions and hard facts with which he enriched his scores of WEA courses.

That is why we are delighted to have received permission from his widow, Hilary, to publish this book. He never had time to illustrate it himself but we have been fortunate enough to be able to draw on the talent of another WEA member, Grace Bevan, to supply this need.

Our publication of this book is our tribute to Basil, to his achievements, his wit, his knowledge and his capacity for friendship from which so many of us have been the beneficiaries.

Arthur Brown

Apples

APPLES

An item in the Essex Review quotes an old farmer on how his "mother used to heat up her wood oven, bake the loaves of bread, then a batch of cakes and pastries, and finally, put in a large bowl full of codlins and leave them there for the night; that is what is meant by 'coddling' – a slow stewing in a mild oven for a long period. We cannot afford the fuel for it nowadays but I can remember delicious fruit of a dark hue in thick syrupy sauce which used to be coddled in this way and eaten with cream".

John Ray, the great botanist of Black Notley, said in his Catalogue of English Plants of 1670 that the Great Willow Herb was called Codlings & Cream from the smell of the flowers and of the leaves a little bruised, like the smell of codlin apples which have been coddled or stewed in pans overnight in ovens first used for bread.

What can one say after these two items? Faggot ovens are a far cry from microwaves; but those with Aga cookers or any cooking device with a slow oven can get close to these delights.

Codlins were a large type of cooking apple with a conical shape at one end and were popular in East Anglia. Essex has produced two notable dessert apples : the D'Arcy Spice said, justly, by Taylor to be much prized as an eating apple for February-March, and the Sturmer Pippin said to have been raised in the 1840s by crossing a Claygate Pearmain with a Ribston Pippin. Yet the most intriguingly named apple was Suffolk's Belliborion said by Forby in 1830 to be a "fine sonorous corruption of the French 'belle et bonne' ". I was also interested when reading Spike Mays 'Reubens Corner' to find that one of his characters mentioned the Blenheim Orange as a really great apple and many locals would agree with him. The Blenheim is a poor cropper some years but it stores and is excellent as eater and cooker. Apples were not quite so seasonal a crop as most fruit because they would store. When they were plentiful, apple puddings were cooked as the main course; and apple jacks or turnovers were special treats.

Edward Moor (1823) describes Suffolk Apple Jacks: sugared apples baked without pan, in a square thin piece of paste with opposite corners 'turned on' the apple or 'flapped' so as to form a turnover or flapjack. Shakespeare has "Thou shalt go home with me and we'll have flesh – and moreover puddings and flapjacks and thou shalt be welcome". Apple Hoglins mentioned by Mrs Osmond in 1903 as being a North Suffolk dish were also a type of flapjack. "Mother wrapped the pastry all round the apple as if she was doing up a parcel", was how one of my 90-year-old contributors described them.

The great question mark against the potential bride, you remember, was can she bake an apple pie? And how many husbands have caused amusement, if not offence, by frequent harkings back to MOTHER'S apple pie. The Norfolk born poet John Loveday remembers apple puddings as an attractive and important part of his childhood diet. His father was the last in a line of threshing engine contractors in Old Buckenham. John slightly preferred the ones his mother made in a basin to the ones cooked in a cloth. Although they were the second course rather than the first, they were the main course as far as he was concerned. Puddings receive their due attention throughout this book.

The apple will stand many treatments: suet or bread-dough puddings, tarts, pies, fritters and 'dumplings'. The last were made by folding shortcrust pastry round peeled cored whole apples filled with brown sugar and sultanas and then baked.

The apple chooses itself to begin this book because the latter is arranged alphabetically but its intrinsic importance makes this additionally appropriate. My wife loves apples, handles them with appreciation and invests the word itself with a kind of mystery and magic. I leave you to ponder the apple's part in classical and religious legend.

For the main recipe I have chosen a 19th century dish from Coggeshall. It's a rather richer one than many families would have afforded.

MRS TELFORD'S APPLE PUDDING   Have ready stewed 12 large apples, flavoured with lemon, nutmeg and sugar. Then take 1 lb of flour, 1 tablespoon baking powder, 4 tablespoons of loaf sugar powdered, ¹/₂ lb butter, 2 well beaten eggs and 3 or 4 tablespoons of milk. Make into a crust. Line the dish, put the apples in, cover with the paste and bake in a brisk oven. When cold turn it out and serve with sifted sugar.

My own strong childhood memory about apples is of those pre-war autumn weekends when everyone was busy in their gardens and orchards. Out would come the ladders, the old galvanised baths, the boxes, the old enamel slop pails and the clothes baskets for that harvest. Boys at this one time of year were actively encouraged to climb trees by their elders.

The wife of the schoolmaster at Newport in Essex mentions in the late 17th century a sweet called "Quoddled Pippins or White Quinces". That satisfyingly brings us back to coddling which began this section; but to conclude it I give you a recipe of 1643 which was given to me when I was lecturing at Gosfield:

TO MAKE APPLE CREAM   Take 12 pippens, pare and slit them, then put them in a skillet and some Claret Wine and a race (root) of ginger shred thin, and a little Lemon cut small and a little sugar, let all these stand together till they be soft; then take them off and put them in a dish till they be cold. Then take a quart of cream boiled with a little nutmeg a while, then put in as much of the Apple stuffe to make of it what thickness you please and to serve it up.

Batter

BATTER

Sunday lunch during my Essex childhood often began with the batter pudding and gravy before we had the meat and vegetables. My grandparents were used to this way and gently checked my mother if she called it Yorkshire rather than batter. This tradition of eating it first must have arisen to help fill up the diners and cut down on the amount of meat required. The practice is confirmed for us by Harry Jordan who was Vicar of Finchingfield. He died in 1968 and the following comes in one of his recently published verses

> In Essex, customs still survive
> Which from a distant past derive.
> One starts with puddings steeped in gravy
> And, eaten with a spoon, Lord save me.

Throughout this book comes the message loud and clear that our ordinary forebears in this region ate very simply, had very little meat and lived largely on puddings, vegetables and bread. Most of the puddings were of the suet or bread dough variety. Batter pudding, because it contained an egg, was a little more high flown, whereas dumplings were a cheaper filling food.

Mary Norwak tells us that the BONX meant beat the batter for the pudding. This sound is close to Cronk which my mother used with the same meaning. As a little boy I used to like to watch her cooking, particularly when she cronked the batter. "Dolly Cronk. Dolly Cronk" we used to chant together in imitation of the sound made by her wooden spoon knocking the sides of the white glazed earthenware basin. It was for me a half magic incantation which made the batter taste better. I saw in my mind's eye a picture of a benign, aproned Dolly Cronk who I took to be the inventor or perhaps the goddess of batter. Mother made the batter first, of course, before the other Sunday dinner preparations, so that it could stand. What little was left in the mixing bowl went into the gravy.

The recipe taught to an Edwardian school child in Essex on 12th April 1910, was

BATTER PUDDING $^1/_4$ lb flour, pinch of salt, 1 egg, $^1/_2$ pint of milk. Put flour and salt in a basin. Beat the egg well and add milk to it. Add the egg and milk by degrees. Leave to stand for a long time before use. (Thick batter for coating fish, etc, use 1 egg to $^1/_4$ pint of milk.)

Charles Clark, a tenant farmer in Totham, published his Essex dialect poem about Tiptree Races in 1840. When his old couple wanted a special dish with some meat for Race Day, they chose one still familiar today.

> A dinner nice the oad folks have
> At race-time, ollus 'ood
> That day they had a toad-in-hole
> A dish that's deadly good.
> But when oad Styles to goffle it
> Bargun, he soon did cry out –
> "Missus! I thinks as how, taa day,
> You've put the meller's eye out!"

She had offended the miller (and her husband) by using too little flour and getting a sloppy mixture but she excused herself quickly by saying that the servant girl had not made the oven hot enough. She had failed to 'rassle' it.

TOAD IN THE HOLE (Essex 1910)   Cut up cooked meat or raw sausages, place in baking tin which contains melted fat. Pour over the batter and bake in a hot oven for $1/2$ or $3/4$ of an hour. I think it's better with the sausages cooked first.

Norfolk liked pieces of liver dipped in batter and fried in 'biling' fat; and its Kidneys in Batter was a variety of Toad in the Hole. Kidneys, skinned and cored, were soaked in salted water and then almost cooked in a baking tin with fat. The batter was poured over before cooking was completed in a hot oven. And, of course, fish in batter is legendary. Some batter recipes separated the yolk and white of the eggs when the batter was for sweet puddings (poured over stuffed apples for instance). Then the white was folded in just before use.

My son, Toby, who is the Chef of an Aldeburgh hotel where they grow their own herbs, tried a new use of batter for starters on us the other day. He coated Sorrel leaves in it and crisped them in deep oil. Not so filling as my mother's batter pud but pleasantly piquant. No doubt the reader will be pleased to have an example of new as well as old cuisine. Incidentally, *pace* Jordan, we did not eat our first course of batter with a spoon back in the thirties. Some of the batter puddings were boiled rather than baked, however, so a spoon may have been the correct implement for them. I therefore give here a 19th century Essex recipe from the Gardner family recipe book.

BATTER PUDDING   8 oz flour of flour half a teaspoonful of baking powder, two eggs and a PINT OF MILK. Mix the flour with the baking powder, a pinch of salt, beat the eggs and then add them, then the milk by degrees. Boil 1$\frac{1}{2}$ hours.

Henry Laver, an Essex doctor, writing in 1902, said of earlier years that when skim milk was a penny a quart and eggs 20 to 24 for a shilling, the Essex agricultural worker's supper table (his supper was often his dinner) was frequently graced with a large batter pudding. Pudding bags were used instead of expensive earthenware basins in which to cook the puddings. The bags were made about a foot long, rather smaller at the bottom for convenience in turning them out. To pour the batter into the bag it was necessary to hold it upright with its mouth open. For this a pudding maid was used. It was a small three legged stool placed seat downwards. The bag was impaled on the sharp points of the legs, permitting one person to pour. A clothes horse was called a clothes maid on the same principle.

Laver added a poignant footnote, "The labourers' wives no longer make batter puddings, the increased cost of eggs having materially interfered with the manufacture of this useful and wholesome article of food". Other less expensive puddings continued to feed the labourers' families, however, and for these see the section on puddings.

Birds

BIRDS

   Several of my informants have told me what you said if anyone was carrying a bird, dead or alive: "If you met a mate carrying something interesting by the legs, you said, 'If that poor creature needs a home, you know where I live' ".

   When our two boys were young, we had a hen on a settin' of eggs. When they hatched, three-quarters of them were cockerels. They grew to be very beautiful and very fierce. Just before Christmas it was impossible to suggest to the family that they be killed and eaten. The Rector, our friend and neighbour, came to the rescue. One morning the cockerels had all gone. When Richard and Toby asked him what had happened to them they were very satisfied with the explanation:

"My dears, everyone of them has gone to good homes in the parish". One of the homes was our own although they didn't realise it. The travelling butcher from Cavendish called in at the Rectory on his way to us and collected an oven-ready bird. He then delivered it to us instead of our usual weekend joint. My wife was unaccountably off meat that weekend but the male members of the family enjoyed it.

Until the recent advent of mass produced birds, chicken had been throughout history a special treat and rarely appeared on the tables of ordinary people. Now that they are eating it all sorts of finger-licking coatings and additions have to be given to it to give it any flavour at all. The rarity of bowling fowl is particularly regrettable. Stuffed (but with enough room inside for the herb or fruit mixture to expand) and then stewed or steamed, after they had been rubbed with lemon juice, they were excellent.

In 1768 a newspaper reported that thieves had broken into a house in Cambridgeshire and, before stealing anything, had regaled themselves with pigeon pye. Elaborate and surprisingly large dovehouses did, of course, provide the big house with a ready supply of tasty meat. Pigeons, if not too old, can be roasted with a little bacon on their breasts. If they seem tough they can be casseroled; or alternatively, simmered first before putting them in a pastry pie with small pieces of bacon or ham and the gravy produced by the first simmer.

A recipe of 1609 suggests boiling pigeons in mutton broth having put herbs inside them. They were served with rice flavoured with mace and lemon juice. I haven't tried it but it sounds good.

Shooting rooks was a job for the gamekeeper early in May. Boys also climbed for them to take them from the nest just before they flew. Only the young ones were eaten. They were skinned, the heads cut off, drawn and the backbone cut out. The pies which followed contained, as well as the rook meat, steak and hard boiled eggs. They were topped with fat bacon before puff paste was put on. Wasn't that a dainty dish to set before a king?

Stewing game birds in a pot was often the method used by legitimate consumers as well as being the traditional way of cooking them by poachers and gypsies. Do you remember the smell of that cooking pot while Toad was selling his horse to a gypsy?

PARTRIDGE STEW   First obtain a brace of partridges, then fry them in dripping or butter. The stewing should be done very slowly. A little chopped bacon or ham, a tomato, perhaps a few mushrooms and your own taste in seasoning should be in the pot with them. Anon.

The artificial rearing of pheasants, feeding them only for the shoot when they are expected to behave like wild pheasants, seems to me a strange form of sport; but, however despatched, they taste good. We go now, however, to a different sort of hunt. Phil Rowe of Bulmer (born 1900) told me about sparrows for food: "Every farmer used to pay a farthing a sparrow to get rid of 'em. My dad made a big net to catch 'em for his brother. They needed two high poles and three men, one on one side of a hedge, one with a stick and the other with a light. He charged 'em seven and six for the net. They went to Armsey and earned the money the first night. Seven and six – a few sparrers eh? They used to eat 'em in pies. Fiddlin' though, just a little bit of meat on the breast".

There follows a 17th century Essex way of cooking small birds like larks and sparrows: Cut off the heads and legs and boil, scum and put therein large mace, white wine, currants well picked and washed, dates, marrow, pepper and salt. Being well stewed, dish them. Thicken the broth with strained almonds, rosewater and sugar. Garnish with lemon, barberries and grated bread.

This came from the wife of the Master of the Free School at Newport. She wrote books "stored with all manner of receipts" between 1667 and 1672. The earlier centuries, it is often suggested, liked their flesh masked with an incredible number of flavourings. A recipe like the one above certainly bears this out.

Be careful with your carving and service. A 17th century warning, based on local observation, follows: "I have seen the good gentlewoman of the house sweat more in cutting up of a fowl than the cook-maid in roasting it; and when she had soundly beliquored her joints, hath suckt her knuckles, and to work with them again in the dish!"

Bread
Puddings

BREAD PUDDINGS

These delicious, filling puddings surely deserve a small section to themselves. You will find the other sweet puddings have one nearer the end of the book. In this we are in the business, not for the last time, of using up not so fresh bread (also see Sops). Remembering that the home baking took place about once a week, several of my oral historians said that the loaves did keep but that they were pretty stale by the end of it.

BREAD PUDDING I (Essex)   Take about $^1/_2$ lb of bread, break it up into pieces and soak them in water for some time. Take off any water not absorbed and beat up with a fork to get out the lumps. Stir in 2 oz of suet, about $^1/_4$ lb of dried fruit, 3 oz of brown sugar and a little spice and mix up well together. Then add an egg beaten in a little milk. Put all of the mixture into a greased dish and bake for about an hour.

The Norfolk recipe which follows was given to me by a Manningtree WEA student. In Norfolk, Nelson's birthplace, said my informant, bread pudding was sometimes known as Nelson Cake or alternatively Nelson Slices. The latter reminds us that bread pudden was good eaten cold in slices, indeed was usually eaten that way.

BREAD PUDDING II   Take eight thick slices of bread at least a day old, break them up in a bowl, pour over half a pint of milk and leave for about half an hour. Then beat till smooth. Add 12 oz dried fruit, 2 oz chopped peel and a grated apple. Stir in 3 tablespoons of soft dark brown sugar, a little orange marmalade, $1^1/_2$ oz of self raising flour, 2 eggs beaten, 1 teaspoon of lemon juice, 1 teaspoon of ground cinnamon and 2 of mixed spice. Melt 4 oz of butter and add to the mixture and beat well. Spread into a greased tin and pour remaining melted butter over the surface. Bake slowly for two hours and then in a hotter oven for a further 20 minutes.

CAKE

"There's cake for tea" or "I've knocked up a little sponge" are welcome remarks to hear and it's still birthday cake not birthday anything else. "If I knew you were coming I'd have baked a cake" underlines the point.

Suffolk provides the most interestingly titled cake I have ever come across. This was GROANING CAKE which was specially made for the lying in of women. Whether the nuss, who helped with "the putting of women to bed" and the subsequent birth, also did the cooking is not mentioned. Certainly the old nuss or midwife sometimes did cook for families for a day or two until the mother was ready to resume her duties. Alas I can find no recipe for Groaning Cake. Can anyone help? DUMB CAKE is, however, mentioned by Forby in his 'The Vocabulary of East Anglia' for 1820. It was made on St Mark's Eve by girls who wanted to have a vision of their future sweetheart. An eggshell full of salt and the same quantities of wheatmeal and barley meal were baked before the fire a little before 12 o'clock at night. The maker had to be alone, fasting and say nothing. "At 12 o'clock the sweetheart will come and turn the cake. The door must be left open for a reason pretty obvious."

The making of SEED CAKE is of great antiquity and is mentioned by Tusser in his 500 Points of Good Husbandry as a necessary accomplishment for Tudor housewives, to be served especially after wheat sowing. Another special occasional use for seed cake is implied in an alternative Suffolk and Norfolk name for it, FUNERAL CAKE. The recipe comes from Coggeshall in Essex but the Suffolk ones in my collection are almost identical.

SEED CAKE   1 lb of flour, 1 lb butter, $3/4$ lb of sifted loaf sugar (caster), 3 or 4 oz of Caraway seeds, 6 eggs. Beat the butter to a cream, dredge in the flour, add the sugar. Beat the eggs separately. Put the eggs in last and beat all together for ten minutes. Line the tin with greased paper. Bake for two hours.

Marjorie Felton (born 1904) helps us to make the point that the popularity of seed cake went on into our own century. Her father, a horseman at Little Maplestead, was very fond of it at tea time. By the thirties, however, some of my younger informants had turned against it. This is the way of new generations.

I can vouch for the delicious nature of Essex Apple Cake because it was cooked to bring to the taste-in of one of my WEA classes by a Shalford housewife in 1985.

ESSEX APPLE CAKE   8 oz apples, peeled, cored and finely chopped. 5 oz sultanas, ¹/₄ pint milk, 6 oz soft brown sugar, 6 oz of self raising flour, 6 oz wholemeal flour, 1 teaspoon mixed spice, 6 oz butter or margarine – melted, 1 egg – beaten, 1 oz Demerara sugar. Mix together the apple, sultanas, milk and sugar. Sieve together the flours and spice. Melt the butter and pour it on to the flour mixture, mix together. Add the fruit mixture and beaten egg, mix well together. Place in a greased and lined 8" x 10" tin. Sprinkle the Demerara over the top. Bake at 325°F for approx 1 hour.

CAMBRIDGESHIRE APPLE CAKE is a tart with pastry at the bottom, then cake or biscuit crumbs followed by apple cooked to a pulp with sugar and lemon. The whole was covered with pastry and sprinkled.

While I was still at Bulmer School we held an Evening of Local Country Food. One of the parents, Rona Nice, had married into the Nice family of Gestingthorpe who have been blacksmiths there for generations, and she sent me a fruit loaf recipe. She said "Mrs Rippingale used to make this for the cake stall at the Church Fete". You can have no better provenance than that and Rippingale is, of course, another famous Gestingthorpe name. There were Rippingales turning out splendid cooking and storage pots there in the 17th century.

MRS RIPPINGALE'S FRUIT LOAF   8 oz sugar, 1 lb dried fruit, 1 cup of warm tea, 1 egg, 1 tablespoon marmalade, 1 lb of self raising flour, 1 teaspoon of mixed spice. Steep dried fruit with the sugar and the cup of tea in a basin overnight. Next day stir in the egg, marmalade, flour and spice. Line two loaf tins with greased paper, cook in moderate oven for 1³/₄ or 2 hours. Cut when cold and butter it.

The cake sections of the village show always ensured a slow and longing progress past them when I was a boy. I sometimes find myself close to doing the same thing 50 years later by spending too long near the cake stall at Church Fetes and Bring & Buys. After speaking to an Essex WI group recently I was asked, as is the custom, to judge the competition. It was for the best Victoria Sponge. I took my time and I insisted, of course, on tasting each one before making my judgment. I knew this was the right thing to do because the sponges of my family and female elders always came back from the village show with a thin slice out.

The words "home-made cake" have a fine quality ring to them and I propose to furnish this section with a comment illustrating the region's attitude to BOUGHT cakes. Dorothy Lewing has been visiting chiropodist over the past 40 years in the villages round Gosfield. One of her patients had been out shopping to buy a shop cake and said afterwards, "It wasn't like the one they shew for show, like".

CHEESE

The ploughman poet Bloomfield said that Suffolk Cheese "like the oaken shelf whereon 'tis laid, mocks the weak efforts of the bending blade". Cassell's 19th century 'Dictionary of Cooking' explains this hardness: "There are cases in which dairy farmers skim the milk before they begin to make cheese. These cheeses are remarkable for their hardness, because caseine, independently of the butter, is an exceedingly hard substance; and these cheeses are sometimes brought into the market and they are so hard that they are the subject of many a joke. Of such are the Suffolk bang cheeses made by frugal housewives in that county, who first take the butter and send it to market and then make their cheese".

Before continuing the saga of Suffolk Bang or Thump it is worth mentioning that Essex had a different reputation. During the mediaeval period the Essex marshes provided grazing for ewes whose milk was used to make very large cheeses. It is known that Essex "chesye" was exported to France.

The strength of Essex cheese is celebrated by one of Skelton's Surrey sluts who brought some as payment for Elinour Rumming's ale.

> She was somewhat foul
> Crooken-necked like an owl,
> And yet she brought her fees,
> A cantle of Essex cheese,
> Was well a foot thick
> Full of maggots quick:
> It was huge and great,
> And mighty strong meat
> For the devil to eat:
> It was tart and pungete!

Farmers' wives and housewives made cows' milk cheese, of course, throughout the centuries. Trip was a new soft cheese made of milk not cream. One method for new milk cheese added a little rennet in water to the milk, still warm from the cow. When set it was drained and pressed in moulds which could drain. It needed several days to dry out. Wonmill was made with flet (skimmed milk) though we are not told about its hardness.

In 1768 Arthur Young said cheese was being made and sold at Castle Hedingham for 3¹/₂d a pound. In the following century the Steeple Bumpstead region had something of a reputation for cheese.

Today's Calluna Farm products (sheep's milk cheese and yogurt) from Hollesley near Woodbridge, are worth seeking out and can be found in health food shops in the region.

It is impossible not to return to Suffolk Bang or Thump, however, because it has aroused so many tributes. 'The Suffolk Garland' has this story, "A parcel of Suffolk Cheese was packed in an iron chest and put on board a ship bound to the East Indies. The rats allured by the scent, ate through the chest but could not penetrate the cheese".

A local rhyme was,

Those who made me were uncivil
For they made me harder than the divil
Knives won't cut me, fire won't sweat me,
Dogs bark at me, but can't eat me.

And the final testimonial? "Good for wheels for wheelbarrows."

DRIPPING and other fats

Jack Allen of Great Bardfield (born 1901) said that his father kept pigs "and there was so much fat on the pigs, you got basins and basins of dripping. Dripping on bread used to be a lot of our food really. Mother baked once a week. We had a bellyful but that's all you can say. People, today, would sneer their nose up at what we ate – apple peels sometimes. Men ate bread and sometimes cheese but usually dripping. There were some men that 'ud rather have their beer than food. My mother had the washing and the baking for all us kids and she used to goo on the land or goo picking too".

Ruth Whybrow (born 1897) of Nayland and Halstead, remembered going gleaning in the fields all day "with a bottle of water and a parcel of bread and dripping for our meal. We got as brown as berries and it was like a holiday to us as we never saw the sea in those days. The butcher tried down his pork fat to get his lard which was pure and like pork dripping to us. I think, as a child, I had more bread and lard than butter as mother could only afford the lard".

When meat was cooked on or in front of the fire, bread dipped in the latch pan which caught the drippings from the meat, was highly prized; but we return to this later in the section on sops. Roasting in ovens still permits us to take off the

fat and keep it before making the gravy with the juices, even though the joints are no longer cooked before the fire. Both my grandmothers liked dripping toast and in this, like countless others, they showed their pleasure and good taste in keeping going a meal that was no longer a necessity between the wars. For my mother, however, it was bread and butter. She always maintained that she would have been quite happy to live on it to the exclusion of practically all other food. The daughters of David Coe, a Gestingthorpe shoemaker, gave me their memories of service in an Essex farmhouse from 1913. The eldest was born in 1900 and her sister (Mrs Clapham) one year later. When they revisited that farmhouse in the 70s, by courtesy of Robert Nott, they reminisced about the problems of being in service: scrubbing brick floors, blackleading stoves, avoiding rats in the kitchen, long hours (one Sunday off a month) and cold attics (which meant sleeping two to a bed was an advantage). Miss Coe's memory of food in service at that time, however, was favourable: "We had 1 lb of farm butter each a week. Nothing had preservatives. It was all fresh".

Many of the country recipes contain large amounts of lard. To us, full of today's thoughts about the dangers of too much fat, they seem alarming amounts; but if you spent 10 or 12 hours working very hard in the harvest field or hand made 1,200 bricks a day, then presumably you burnt this fat up.

P. H. Emerson, the Norfolk realist photographer wrote about the farm workers' harvest cake. He said it was "a cake, with currants in it, made with plenty of lard, for this bait. He could smell it through the sacking".

Whether or not hard work burnt up fat, many of today's older country people that I have interviewed are convinced that their diet around the turn of the century was healthier than the one they follow today. Good bread, allotment grown vegetables and nourishing puddings were the staple foods with a change of fish or, even rarer, a little meat. When I talked to a stroke patients' Club at a Sudbury hospital, several of the men, who had grown crops or cared for meat animals in the countryside round about, were adamant that the food of their youth was healthier and less adulterated.

EGGS

John Howlett, the vicar of Great Dunmow, wrote in 1788, " . . . eggs, chicken, etc have never been of any great consequence to the Poor". Furthermore it doesn't do to think that the families of the smaller, working farmers had a diet flowing with eggs, cream and honey. Working farmers' wives kept hens and worked in the dairy but a lot of the milk was skimmed for butter that was sold and most of the eggs were sold too. Between the two world wars milk, butter and eggs provided an important part of the farm income. A good deal of the land was down to grass unlike East Anglia's intensively arable post-war acres.

In the Edwardian period eggs were not readily available for ordinary families. "We sometimes had half an egg for our Sunday breakfast" said a woman born in 1899; another remembered "going nine children to three eggs, your share was spooned on to bread"; "grandmother was the wife of a Rivenhall horseman and had ben a cook in service, she looked after the farm poultry so cracked eggs from the poultry yard were sometimes available (early 1900s)".

Take six eggs is the often used phrase in Mrs Beeton but she was writing for the Victorian middle class and all the foregoing about using cracked eggs and sharing one egg reflects the reality of egg scarcity; but there were some early enthusiasts for going to work on an egg. Great Bentley's Herb Taylor was recorded at 86 years of age by the late much lamented Carl Morton of the Essex Dialect Society: "When I got married I lived on one o' they back housen. For breakfast I useter hev nuthin' but bread and marge or marmalade but I allus had a raw egg in my second cup of tea. I had to get up early to get steam up time I worked on the machine (for threshing tackle). I still do that now and I reckon that's what made me keep so well all the time I was outside".

After the first war chicken farming became popular for those with a bit of money to risk and these farms began to make eggs more widely available. Since the last war we have had factory farming with intensive egg and broiler units which have made eggs cheaper but public distaste for its products and its methods is obviously growing all the time.

Egg custard was greatly in favour, I seem to remember, among the cooks of my family. One of my aunts was so fond of it that when we visited her this was the expected pudding and our expectations were invariably fulfilled. Custard powder was frowned upon (as were Camp coffee, tinned beans and shop cake). With all of us, I suspect, there are things for which we must thank our upbringing.

We all have our own egg preferences. I look upon well-scrambled eggs as a definite delicacy. Beat the eggs a little, add a little milk, season and pour into a pan in which you have melted a little butter. When they begin to set, out with them on to the toast. Mrs Beeton suggests a sprinkling of parsley before serving. Each occasion that I enjoy them gradually obliterates the less happy memory of the wartime variety made with dried egg.

FROGS

Dixon Smith in his 'Finchingfield Tales' mentions an Essex man who was fond of small frogs with which he refreshed himself while hedging and ditching. Hindes Groome, the parson at Earl Soham, wrote more than a century earlier of old Mr Pettee of that place who stuttered and loved to catch small freshers (young frogs) and let them hop down his throat, when he would stroke his stomach, observing "B,b,b,b,-eautifully cool".

Small frogs were eaten also, specifically as a cure. It was believed that they would absorb the corruption within a sick person into their own bodies. It is possible that the expression "frog in the throat" came from this practice of allowing the frog to hop down from the mouth to cure a sore throat.

The most extraordinary story of all about frog eating comes from Norfolk. B. Knyvett Wilson wrote in 1930 about his parson father's memories: "An old villager asserted that he had a living frog in his inside. He had, he said, swallowed it when he (and it) was young in a glass of water and that it had been in his innards ever since. It acted as a barometer. 'Law, maaster, when thass a-goin to rain you should hare him sing, he do fair holler' ".

Swallowing small frogs live, as food or medicine, is a less barbarous business than what I read is done today to provide the legs for fashionable restaurants. I have therefore deliberately omitted any recipe for this section.

Frumity

FRUMITY

When ta rain frummety mind ye heent a dish ta seek. Suffolk Proverb.

The poets had their say too about this ancient dish. Herrick says the hock feast had "several dishes standing by/As here a custard, there a pie/and here all tempting Frumentie". Clare told "How the huge bowl was in the middle set/At breakfast time as clippers yearly met/Fill'd full of frumity where yearly swum/ The streaking sugar and the spotting plumb". The East Anglian Tusser (1523-1580) also rhymed his advice to husbandmen and their wives,

Wife, some time this week if the weather hold cleere
And end of wheat sowing we make for this yeare
Remember you, therefore, though I do it not,
The seed cake, the pasties and Furmentie-pot.

What was it ? Take new or dehusked wheat (pearl barley will do) and soak it for at least 24 hours until the grain has swollen and burst. Then boil it up. You can then bake it overnight in a slow oven or boil it for a couple of hours. Various flavourings were used: sugar, honey, raisins (plumbs) cinnamon, all-spice ,milk; and, sold at the Fairs it contained rum (see Thomas Hardy).

As you have read, the times for eating it varied but Suffolk seems to have preferred Christmas time. Mrs Osmond speaking for N. Suffolk in 1903 said it was baked all night in the oven for the 12 days of Christmas. Forby, about 1820, said large quantities were prepared in High Suffolk farmhouses and the labourers and their wives and children were invited to breakfast upon it on Christmas Day.

It is certainly one of our oldest dishes. The fact that some was placed in a plate outside the door at night for the Pharisees suggests it is pre-Christian. For Pharisees read Fairies in Suffolk; but it had this meaning in Essex as well as place names like Pharisees' Green suggest. Ugley in Essex has a Pharisee's Hole.

A recipe of 1654 gives a frumity variant using barley (Boil till it breaks, change water and boil again). It calls it Pap of Barley, however, a rather less attractive name.

A 16th century version of the Bible (Lev. xxiii 14) reads, "Ye shall eat neither bread, nor parched corn, nor frumenty of new corne until . . . ye have brought an offeringe". But a much later religious connection shows how important this dish was in every day experience. A Suffolk National (Church) School mistress was questioning her charges,

"What did God make on the second day of the Creation ?"

"Please, Maam, he made some furmetty. "

Firmaments were not within her pupil's experience but furmetty certainly was. I have made frumity several times and rather enjoy it. When it has been available for our guests, however, rather a lot has been left.

Fungi

FUNGI

Ruth Whybrow (born 1897) in the course of a delightful long letter to me, written after I had talked to her older persons' group in Halstead, said, "Father made the mushroom ketchup. We had a huge willow patterned dish and he would place the mushrooms upside down and cover them with salt. They used to stand for days till the dish was full of black juice. Then he had to put his spices in after he had strained off the juices . It was very nice and better than what you can buy in the shops today as they were Nature's mushrooms and pure ingredients".

A correspondent from the Brentwood area said her father was also the ketchup maker and that he needed several pounds of mushrooms to make a bottle. It was satisfying to watch him pour his own ketchup over his wife's puddings.

Ruthven Todd, the poet, who lived at one time at Tilty in Essex, wrote an interesting poem about the fungi he found there, "Besides my Essex farmhouse, clustered blewits were palely violet below the dark fruited sloes". Phil Rowe (born 1900) told me a characteristic story about blewits. "When I worked at Upper Houses I picked bushels of bluits. I called them blue stalks. I had them for breakfast every morning for three weeks and I never got sick of them . You give me mushrooms three times a week and I should'a got sick of them, but I never got sick of them bluits. The wife might'a done cooking 'em because of their smell; but still you put up with that sort of thing. Mushrooms cooking is a pleasant smell but bluits were awful." Dorothy Hartley says that bluits should not be fried but stewed so this may possibly explain the Rowe family's problems with cooking them .

I remember one of my elders getting up very early to go mushrooming for his family and saying that fields where cows were on, were the best source. Archie White in his Mersea reminiscences remembered picking field mushrooms to sell as a boy.

Several of my informants have agreed that they like mushrooms best fried until they are crisp. Two insisted that pig's lard should be used for the frying and that fried bread should accompany them.

The recipe comes from Suffolk.

MUSHROOM PUDDING   Line your basin with pastry made from flour and suet. Then fill it with mushrooms together with a small quantity of bacon. Put in a little butter and a little water and cover with more crust. Around two hours steaming is required.

HARES and RABBITS

Jack Allen, who worked on a number of Essex farms after leaving school, had a favourite story which concerned the time-honoured practice of sending the parson a hare or a pheasant after the farmer and his friends had enjoyed a day's sport: "The farmer said to one of the farm boys, 'Take this hare to the Vicar,' Off he went. Vicar came to the door and the boy said, 'Boss sent yer this owd hare,' 'That's not the way to address your vicar. Now then, boy, I'll tell you how to do it. Let's pretend you are me and I am you. I'll tell you how you should address me.' Parson speaking as boy, 'The master sent you this hare with his compliments.' Boy as parson, 'Oh, thank you very much - here's half a crown for yourself' ".

SUFFOLK JUGGED HARE   Wash the hare and cut it into small pieces and flour them. Cover with water and stew till tender with onions, herbs, spice, cloves and seasoning. Having taken out the hare joints thicken the gravy, add a little wine (port perhaps) and cook it again for a little while and sieve it before serving with the pieces of hare. Fruit jelly is a traditional accompaniment. Redcurrant or sloe and crab apple jelly are particularly good.

When I went to visit A. S. Neill's famous school at Leiston in the 1950s I went by train as far as Saxmundham and broke my journey there for a lunch at the Bell Inn. Jugged hare was on the menu; I had it and I still remember it with pleasure. Country hotels and inns have for hundred of years provided meals for the farmers of the district coming in for market day. They ate and drank well. The hare played an important part in folk lore and mythology. There is an excellent book on the

subject by George Ewart Evans and David Thompson. There were some local taboos about eating them and, in any case, those who caught them found it more profitable to sell them than eat them, as they fetched a good price. In 1644 an Essex doctor from Dunmow gave as the cure for convulsions, "Intrales of a hare (heart, liver, lunges) dried to a powder". There wasn't much magic about the rabbit but it was, of course, an important source of meat for the countryman.

I was loaned, by one of my students, the late 19th century journal of a Bradfield St George farmer. He was the son of the family and in his twenties. One of his passions was the new fangled bicycle but he also records much shooting of rabbits, pigeons and sparrows. He attended a stag hunt and often went rat and mole catching. As well as the occasional bit of pork or bacon the country workers also enjoyed "a rarbut or two". Apart from mentioning that country pubs had rabbit nets for hire we won't go into whether they were poached or bought. Certainly, between the wars, the farmers were often glad of the money they got from selling rabbits, caught on their land, for 4d a time.

ESSEX RABBIT PIE   You boil the skinned and washed rabbit with onions and seasoning. Then remove the bones from the meat, add some chopped pork (or sausage meat) and some herbs and put everything into a pie dish. Cover with pastry and bake for about an hour.

"We didn't see any beef when I was young but we had a few rarbuts."

"We had a tidy few rabbit stews and rabbit pies and them last were best cold because of the jelly."

"My dog killed 80 rabbits in one harvest. When he heard the tackle, he wouldn't give us nor peace until I took him up there where they was harvesting." The final recipe dates back to the year 1654:

TO BOIL A RABBIT   Boil them in water and salt. Mince Thyme and Parsley together, a handful of each, boil it in some of the liquor. Then take three of four spoonfuls of verjuyce(Q.V.), a pice of butter, two or three eggs. Stir the eggs together in the liquor, set it upon the fire till it be thick, then pour it upon the rabbet to serve it.

HARVEST CAKES

Clubs, organisations and periodicals have been frequent producers of cookery books by getting their members or readers to send in the recipes. I have read and enjoyed many of them; but the most unusual one was loaned to me by a member of a WEA group and it went back to the days of the Suffragette movement. The Womans Suffrage Cookery Book had a contributor from Geldeston. Her recipes included Norfolk Dumplings and Harvest Buns. The latter were made from bread dough flavoured with fruit and sugar. Keeping back some of the dough that had been made for bread making was a frequent practice. M. Betham Edwards in her Suffolk novel 'The Lord of the Harvest' (1899) says that these harvest cakes were taken with the home-brewed in the harvest field.

" 'Halt for Bever' says the lord. As to the harvestmen, faces grew ruddier, tongues became more loquacious, but, wonderful as it seemed, none got drunk. Each with infinite content munched his hunk of harvest cake, that excellent dough cake, well sugared, spiced and sprinkled with currants made in the shape of small loaves and never seen except during this season."

Fourses cake was another name for it. Lady Gomme said it was yeast bread, lard, currants, sugar and spice and eaten by the harvesters at four o'clock. She took one down from Suffolk and showed it at a Folk Lore Society meeting in London in 1892. Some say it got its name from the time it was eaten and others that it was scored both ways across it to make a four sectioned bun. Some of these Bever cakes were richer, with the addition of lard. This was either mixed in or it was dabbed on strips which were rolled up. The WI's 'Traditional Fare of England & Wales' (1948) has a Suffolk version delightfully titled "Brotherly Love". You took two inch strips of the dough and placed on them small pieces of lard with sugar. Then you rolled them up and baked for about half an hour in a hot oven.

Alan Jobson is good on food in several of his Suffolk miscellanies. His Bever cake is also rich, with lard, eggs, sugar, raisins, peel and nutmeg added to the bread dough. His Fatty Cake was made by continually rolling out the dough, spreading with lard, sprinkling with sugar and folding over.

Eating plenty of these traditional cakes might well produce the remark, "I wholly fare full". One woman remembered as a child going along the tables at the treat to find out which of the buns or cakes seemed to have the most currants in it and then trying to sit opposite it when the time came to get up agin the table.

Mrs Richards passed on to Wrabness WEA's collection a local variant which originally came from Mrs Paskell of Wix. Hodmedods was the name because the finished product looked like a snail.

HODMEDODS   Rollout some short crust pastry (eg surplus from a pie) to make a rectangle about a quarter of an inch thick. Spread a thin layer of soft margarine, then some dried fruit, demerara sugar and a sprinkling of cinnamon. Wet the edges of the pastry and roll up, like a swiss roll. Place on a greased baking tin, with the join underneath. With a sharp knife cut the roll into slices about half an inch thick but leave in position. Bake for about 20 minutes at 350-400°F until pale brown. Leave in the tin until cold before separating the slices.

This time you will have noticed that it is pastry surplus that is used rather than bread dough. There is a Suffolk lullaby in which hodmedods (snails), swiffs (newts), nippadors (stag beetles), meece and clapperclaws are invoked to get the little varmint off to sleep.

As this section seems to have developed into quotes from other persons' cookery collections, I finish it with one of Mary Norwak's versions of these bread cakes from her 'East Anglian Recipes'.

CAKE-IN-THE-PAN-FOR-KATE'S YOUNG-MAN (Suffolk)   1 lb dough; 4 oz currants; 4 oz sugar; 2 oz lard; 1 teaspoonful of spice. Pull the dough as flat as possible. Put in the lard and work it well into the dough. Add the currants and sugar sprinkled with the spice, knead well. Divide into four, pull flat again and place in flat tins. These cakes may be split in half and buttered and jammed, or they may be eaten cold. This is a very old harvest cake.

HERRINGS

The smoking of herring dates back in East Anglia to at least the 13th century. Seven hundred years later Brown (born 1893) told me that the man who sold herrings through the village of Rayne in Essex, had an unusual cry. It was "Hev'em or no, that's my price". Local housewives, when times were hard, were obviously keen to bargain for their change of diet or Saturday treat and this street cry was the result. Both facts illustrate the importance of the herring in the history of the region. A few more items follow to reinforce them.

One of the local phrases collected by the famous John Ray of Black Notley in the 17th century was A YARMOUTH CAPON which turned out to be A RED HERRING – "more herrings being eaten than capons bred here". The Great Bardfield Vestry Minutes record this for April 1718, "The Herring money Paid by Mr Pain according to ye will of Sergeant Bendlowes was distributed to ye poor

according to their several n'cetys in ye presence of us". At Clavering John Thame's will decreed that a barrel of white herrings (pickled herrings) and a cade of red herrings should be given to the local poor each Lent.

W. Lawrence (born 1889) was a Colchester man and said that herrings were the poorer man's meat and that bloaters were therefore called two eyed steaks. At Shalford Walter Harvey (born 1893) said "I can remember Mr. Parry, the sweep, telling my mother that when he married he had *two* bloaters for the wedding breakfast".

The ordinary country dwellers such as farmworkers, weavers, brickmakers and their families ate very little meat. Many of those that I have interviewed, whose childhood was in the last century or very early in this one, say that bread, potatoes and pudding formed the basis of their diet. I deal with these foods under their own separate headings. When there was a change of diet it did not often take the form of meat but of fish, particularly herrings and sprats. The recorders of East Anglian people, like Lilias Rider Haggard, C. Henry Warren and George Ewart Evans, bear this out. The first mentioned quotes a Norfolk gamekeeper for the 1890s, "Scores of famleys were brought up on potatoes, turnips and bread with what was called pork lard and treackle – with a change of herring". Warren's Mark Thurston, born in 1861 in Finchingfield, said that when bloaters were two for three half pence his father and elder brother were at work so got one each whereas he, a boy, "used to toast the bones they left, then suck the juice out of 'em and eat the tail and fins". Evans recorded Annie Gable from the Saxmundham area: "You know when bloaters were 12 a shilling we didn't have a whole one. I used to toss up with my brother to see who'd have the tail. There's more in the head, aint there?"

Dolly Argent remembered that in the early years of the century herrings at a penny each were sold from a bike in Great Maplestead or by "Meadows who sold wet fish from a cart and who had a special whip to dislodge the cats ". The fish sellers who came round the villages were often men who had lost an arm in farm machinery accidents "but could do more with their one than some could wi' two".

Herrings not only fed the less well off in Britain. They were widely exported. One of my WEA students (Mrs E. Page) offered this memory, "During July 1914 I was on holiday with my family at Gt Yarmouth. I still recall being taken into a large place with planks of wood across the floor and a cold pavement to walk round on. Someone lifted up a plank or two and underneath I saw hundreds of silver herring floating around. The fish was being pickled for sale in tubs on the continent". Salted, herrings fed Europe and Russia as well as East Anglia. There are those who maintain that the Vikings arrived here having set out in pursuit of the herring. In mediaeval times men owed service to the Lord of the Manor and an early 14th century record for Essex says that while giving two days ploughing in winter and spring each man had two loaves and six herrings.

Bloaters, which are of course still with us, are herrings salted and then lightly smoked for only about 12 hours, whereas Red Herrings were soaked in brine for two days and nights and then smoked several times with sweating days when there was no fire . This process produced a dried fish of a deep red colour which would keep .

In 1599 Thomas Nashe issued a magnificently wordy hymn of praise to the red herring, saying that "the poorer sort make it three parts of their sustenance" and that "on no coast like ours is it caught in such abundance, no where dressed in his right cure but under our horizon; hoisted, roasted and toasted here alone it is, and as well powdered and salted as any Dutchman would desire." Nashe's final peroration reaches fever point, " My conceit is cast into a sweating sickness with ascending the steps of the Red Herring's renown; into what a hot broiling Saint Laurence's fever would it relapse then, should I spend the whole bag of my wind in climbing up to the lofty mountain crest of his trophies? But no more wind will I spend on it but this: Saint Denis for France, Saint James for Spain, Saint Patrick for Ireland, Saint George for England, and the RED HERRING for YARMOUTH." Nashe was a Lowestoft man .

We have given the fresh herring scant attention so let's return to the earlier years of our own century and the many local families for whom they were a Saturday treat cooked "in a little Dutch oven in front of the fire" or otherwise, and for whom they were "a feast fit for a king." No doubt they came from NasheVille!

Institutional Fare

INSTITUTIONAL FARE

John Howlett, the Vicar of Great Dunmow, was an opponent of changes to the old poor law, "Don't pull down the venerable pile of our general system of Poor Laws. It stands a distinguished monument of the wisdom and humanity of the British Nation." Under the old poor relief system parishes looked after their own poor by raising a local rate. At the end of the 18th century Howlett and others opposed those who wanted Houses of Industry like the ones in parts of Suffolk and Norfolk. These last were forerunners of the later universal Union Workhouses of the 19th century which were the product of the new poor law.

Howlett not only opposed the large workhouses because of their inhuman aspects by quoting astonishing rates of mortality in them; but he also quotes a Norfolk writer on another reason for rejecting them: "Those brought up in Houses of Industry accustomed to the hot atmosphere and kept indoors cannot bear the changes of the weather (so) that they are absolutely unable to pull turnips (when returned to cottage life). The coarse food and hard lodging of the farmer's servants are not equally delicate with that to which they have been accustomed in their Houses of Industry. Farmers refuse boys or young men who have lived in any House of Industry."

This suggests that the labourer's food was coarser than that doled out in these early workhouses catering for a number of parishes. An 18th century Suffolk House of Industry Dietary gave the paupers bread and butter (or cheese) for breakfast from Monday to Saturday and milk broth on Sunday. Their suppers were all of bread and cheese. Their dinners were pease broth on Mondays and Fridays, suet pudding on Tuesdays, milk broth and dumplings on Thursdays, bread and cheese on Saturdays and beef with meal dumplings on Sundays and Thursdays.

The dietary for the Aylsham Union Workhouse for 1845 is given in the excellent collection of source material called "The Poor Law in Norfolk, 1700-1850". Able bodied men had 7 oz of bread and a pint of milk gruel (skilley or very thin porridge) for breakfast every day. Supper was 7 oz of bread with ¾ oz of cheese or ½ oz of butter. For dinner meat pudding with vegetables was provided on two days of the week, the Sunday meal was 9 oz of bread with 1 oz of cheese, Monday's was potatoes and plain suet pudding, Saturday's was vegetables and dumplings and for the remaining days it was vegetables with bread and a little cheese. Women got slightly smaller helpings but the infirm had cooked meat and broth on two days a week, dumplings more frequently and sweetened tea at supper time.

These diets from Suffolk and Norfolk are typical. The Halstead, in Essex, diet board can be seen in the Halstead Bung Chapel Museum. Several commentators have made the point that during the frequent periods of hard times in the countryside folk probably ate better in the workhouse than out of it. Certainly the total amounts of plain food (e.g. 18 oz of bread per day) don't seem too niggardly to us; but you must remember that the able bodied were putting in long hours of hard work in the workhouse and needed plenty of food.

"We do not have food enough to do his hard work," said an Essex lad in 1837 to the Chairman of Guardians at his work house.

The amounts of meat provided in the workhouse varied over the years just as the amount eaten by labourers in their own home varied with prices and the level of their wages.

Those East Anglians who went into the Navy got a coarse and monotonous diet but there was supposed to be much more meat in it than their civilian counterparts were likely to see – a pound of fresh or $^3/_4$ lb of salt beef or pork per day. The daily allowance for vegetables was only half a pound (and that usually pease). The strikers of 1797 "grievously complained" of the lack of vegetables. The quality of the salt meat was highly criticised. The beef and cheese could be carved like wood and the pork was acrid. The least said about ships' biscuits the better.

Lads leaving the workhouse were often advised to join the Army. The story for the soldiers was similar. There was more food than they could easily obtain outside but it was often spoiled in the cooking. One Essex woman enjoyed telling me how her mother saved up something scarce and delicious for her son's return from the 1st World War; but didn't appreciate his reaction when he saw that it was Bully Beef.

William Matthews, born in 1808 in Coggeshall, joined the Army and was in the Guards at Cambridge and London. In his memoirs he has the following item about Barracks food in 1830, "At 12 o'clock all assemble for dinner when every one has a plate set ready for him containing $^3/_4$ lb meat, 1 lb potatoes, $^1/_2$ lb of bread and a basin holding two pints of soup, and I am in honour bound to acknowledge that every article of food is of excellent quality". He thought less highly of the overcrowded barracks and the "effluvia" arising from sweating men.

School dinners were a mid 20th century idea in the countryside. Before this bread and scrape of jam or lard was taken from home by those who lived too far from school to get back home for dinner. School meals provided by local authorities after the war were often nourishing and substantial. I enjoyed a lot of them. The coming of higher charges and fast food from factories which was warmed up, in more recent years, has sent many parents back to packing up sandwiches. My memories of the better school food are of good meat puddings and pies and delicious puddings of the suet or sponge variety with which several skilled school cooks tried to fatten me up over the years. I also have fairly favourable memories of the Second World War's British Restaurants, but then I have never been averse to a bit of stodge.

Whenever I have quoted a Norfolk housewife of 1937 to my audiences, to the effect that her man didn't feel he'd had a dinner unless it had included pudding, there have often been groans of recognition from the women, suggesting that there may still be men about like that.

For your recipe? An early naval one:

SHIPS' BISCUITS   (made of wheat and pea flour and of extreme hardness) pounded up in a canvas bag, and mixed with pork fat and sugar to make a 'cake'.

Invalid Food

INVALID FOOD

John Suckling, of Steeple Bumpstead, told me his memories of his grandmother who was a great supporter of the Congregational Chapel there. She made beef tea to take to those with pneumonia and stayed up late on Saturdays making pasties and buns to leave by the chapel door, on Sunday, for those in need to help themselves to as they left. The depression between the wars had just as much effect as those in late Victorian and Edwardian times. A 19th century book says beef tea should be made by cutting the meat in pieces and cooking it in a covered jar in the oven. The same book mentions the following as suitable food for invalids: sweetbreads, ox tail, beef tea, eggs in tea or sherry, boiled soles, poached eggs, pigeon stewed, calves feet jelly, oysters, partridge or pheasant, boiled custard, boiled bread pudding. It substituted invalid biscuits in milk in place of bread and milk. Some of these sound like rather rich food for the rather rich. An Edwardian recipe book suggests as invalid food, beef tea, port wine lozenges and calf's foot jelly, chicken or mutton broth and rice milk. The calf's foot jelly contained lemons, sugar, whites of eggs, sherry and sometimes brandy so it must indeed have been RESTORATIVE.

A 19th century born Essex farmworker's daughter, however, balances things up with: "Onion gruel was our cure, or bread and milk. They both seemed to do the trick so we didn't miss much schooling".

'Sickroom Cooking' of 1903 reinforces this with, " A drink of gruel or barley water, or whey, going to bed, gives great relief". One of my grandmothers would have said hear hear to this. She was a great one for barley water and thought it was particularly good for tissicks (troublesome coughs). She married a postman whose surname was Cook and she was courted by him while she was cooking at Wivenhoe Park (taken over after the war by Essex University). The big Bible in my bookcase is inscribed "To Martha from Sampson Hanbury, Feb. 12th 1897, Wyvenhoe Park". Lower down among others is recorded the birth of a grandson, Basil, and I think she might have been pleased that he is concocting a book about food. The recipe comes from a dictionary of cooking of the same period as her Bible.

BARLEY WATER   Take two ounces of pearl barley, wash it well, and boil for ten minutes in a little water to clear it. When drained put to it five pints of boiling water and let it boil until reduced to one half. Then strain for use. An excellent pectoral drink is made by boiling the barley as above, and adding the following ingredients: half an ounce of licorice root, sliced and well bruised; two ounces of figs, the same of raisins stoned; distilled water, one pint to one quart of the prepared barley water. Let all boil till the liquid is reduced to two pints, then strain for use. If used freely this preparation will be found very efficacious in cases of inflammatory attacks of the chest, coughs &c. Probable cost 4d. per pint.

A Chigwell recipe suggests flavouring with lemon and sugar (instead of the rather elaborate one above) and this, of course, was common.

Whooping Cough was a great scourge and this demanded more impressive cures than barley water. One Essex recipe book suggests cutting some garlic, soaking it in rum or gin and then rubbing the chest and spine with it night and morning. A more frequently met with remedy for whooping cough was to eat a boiled or fried mouse. I have met two ladies in my WEA classes who were treated this way. One of them was from Suffolk and the other from Essex. Labourers made tea from pieces of toasted bread; and a sickroom recipe (1903) designed to cure THIRST was: TOAST WATER, Toast well but do not burn some pieces of crusty bread, put into a quart jug, fill with boiling water, strain when cold. The same source recommends apple water and rhubarb water (slice fruit, add sugar, lemon rind and boiling water, cover till cold and strain).

When a person was ill (or pregnant) and fancied some nourishment the word used was often 'linger'. "How I do linger for . . .". Pudden possibly?

INFANT OR INVALID PUDDING (late 19th century)   Take a tea cup of very fine bread crumbs and two teacups of milk poured boiling over. When the crumbs have soaked, heat up half an egg and mix with it. (A whole egg for an older person). Pour into a jar, tie over, and boil in a saucepan for two hours. Sweeten or serve with gravy.

JAMS and JELLIES

Bread and a scrape of jam was what many country school children of the region took for their school dinner, washed down by water from the pump or the well. A lot of them had too long a walk to school for going back home at midday to be possible.

A simple country jam made in East Anglia was Free Jam. The free comes from the fact that it makes use of blackberries and elderberries, equal quantities of the two fruits, $^3/_4$ lb of fruit to 1 lb of sugar. Blackberries were picked in both world wars to help the war effort. In 1918 Bulmer school children picked 699½ lb to help feed the nation. I like the precision of that 699½ entry in the School Log book. Accuracy was more important than rounding off to 700. Womens Institutes made a great deal of jam and bottled surplus fruit in their village centres. I can remember my mother and the other Wivenhoe WI members bottling and jamming everything within sight at their centre near the Cross. A recent Essex WI News had a marvellous account of Little Maplestead's efforts and eventual failure to set up a centre. Margery Allingham also said that she overheard two Tolleshunt d'Arcy women at the beginning of the 1939 war as they went past her open window. One of them said "I'd rather let me fruit rot than let the Women's Institute get their hands on it".

Rose hip and apple jam was also made in Essex. The hip juice was strained through muslin first. Damsons are not as easy to get hold of as they were earlier in the century and a lot of cottage bullace trees and bullace hedges have been cut down. Ruth Whybrow said, " We had a bullace tree in our garden at Nayland. They were a white fruit, the size of a damson. Father used to make the jam and we enjoyed that while it lasted." For Damson Cheese the fruit needs to be softened slowly in a slow oven until the stones are free, then they are stirred and rubbed through a sieve. Some of the stones are cracked and the kernels added. Using 1 lb of sugar to 1 lb of pulp the mixture is boiled to jelling point. The cheese is better kept for some months. Whole or halved quinces can be cooked in this way and sieved to make a cheese or jam, but lemon juice should be added.

Since I retired I have made a lot of jam and jelly. I think my own favourite jam is FOUR FRUIT jam combining blackcurrants, gooseberries, logan berries and raspberries. These ripen close enough usually to use fresh fruit; but they all freeze and mine is often made after Christmas. The gooseberries and blackcurrants need a lot of softening before the logan berries and finally the raspberries go in.

JELLIES

Partly to avoid the pip problem jelly was often made. For many years my wife Hilary used to get the crab apples from the school hedge and make a very popular jelly for the annual sale. I think the best jelly of them all is SLOE AND APPLE JELLY. You take roughly equal weights of sloes and apples. The 1987 sloes were magnificent, round and full like small plums. Cut up the apples without peeling or coring, just cover all the fruit with water in the pan and simmer until soft. After straining through the jelly bag, use the usual pint of juice to a pound of sugar, stir till the sugar is melted and make the final rapid boil up. The sloes give it an exceptional flavour. It can be eaten on bread or toast or used as an accompaniment to meat.

For QUINCE JELLY cut up the quinces and simmer in enough water to cover them. Drip through a jelly bag and use one pint of juice to one pound of sugar. Cinnamon makes it more spicy.

MARMALADE

Essex has a reputation for good commercially made marmalades and jams by Wilkins of Tiptree. Maura Benham's 'The Story of Tiptree Jam' (1985) tells the story well with the aid of many fascinating photographs.

The old marmalade recipe I give is for lemon marmalade and it comes from Great Cornard in Suffolk.

LEMON MARMALADE: Take any number of lemons and slice them very thinly. Remove just the pips. Add 3 pints of cold water to each lb of fruit and let it stand for 24 hours. Boil the fruit until tender and let it stand again in a bowl until the next day. To every lb of boiled pulp add 1 lb of sugar, boil all together till it jellies. The slices of lemon will look rather transparent. When taking out the pips, be careful to leave in all the white pith as this helps to make the syrup.

Since we started growing our own quinces I have found what an excellent marmalade they make. They were used for this purpose, apparently, before oranges appeared on the scene in any quantity.

QUINCE MARMALADE You peel and core (there is a lot of core) the quinces, slice the pieces thinly and simmer them for quite a long time until soft, The customary pound of sugar to a pound of fruit is used and the juice of a lemon added with the sugar improves the flavour and setting.

As an Essex schoolboy in the 30s I can remember that when friends played together in each other's gardens or homes the host mum would provide elevenses. One family were wealthier than us (they ran a car!) but my mother after asking once what I had for elevenses was surprised that it had been bread and marmalade without butter. She herself always spread her home-made marmalade on the bread but, despite the fact that times were hard, she made it a matter of pride to manage a scrape of butter between the marmalade and the bread. Marmalade not jam of course. The poor ate bread and jam.

Let's leave these strange social distinctions and return to the Second World War. Lilias Rider Haggard in Norfolk heard a dripping noise in the cupboard and realised they had a flood. "Had it or had it not reached the most precious of all our possessions – not pictures, first editions, or clothes but the SUGAR FOR THE JAM. A tap had been left running but we saved the sugar".

In the Basildon area blackberries, elderberries, crab apples and sloes were combined to make a TONIC JAM. With those four free fruits the flavour must have been outstanding; and I am quite prepared to believe it made you feel better. All good things do.

KITCHELS

Wright's English Dialect Dictionary gives: "Kichel, Suffolk, a flat cake manufactured on New Year's Eve" or Christmas, of triangular shape with sugar and a few currants over the top. Wright appears to have got his information from Moor (1823) whose definition is the same but adds that the word is Saxon and that God's Kichels were given to God children.

Kitchels are mentioned in Chaucer's Canterbury Tales in the 14th century but most of the references to them that I have come across have mentioned the particular Suffolk practice of having some of these little cakes ready when the god children visit their god parents at Christmas time and ask for a blessing.

Leslie Weaver, Harwich's historian, gave some interesting detail to my WEA class in Harwich. It appears that, until 1949, Mayor's Day in Harwich was 21st December, the beginning of the season for giving kitchels, and it became the custom for the newly elected Mayor to shower his blessings on the children by throwing kitchels to them from a window at the Guildhall. When this began is not known but a guide book in 1905 described it as a curious custom, hundreds of years old and thought the cakes were called "catch alls".

Allan Jobson in his 'Aldeburgh Story' claims that Aldeburgh was the home of Kitchel Cakes. He says that they had to be baked on New Year's Eve and eaten before midnight as bad luck would come to those who ate after the New Year had dawned. Mr. Weaver's recipes for Kitchels follows and if you feel like making them on New Year's Eve, remember that in East Anglia it was traditional to drink spiced elderberry wine while eating these triangular blessing cakes. They are delicious and with the wine they must be irresistible.

KITCHELS   1 lb puff pastry; 8 oz currants; 3 oz chopped candied peel; 2 teaspoon cinnamon; 1 teaspoon ground nutmeg; 2 oz ground almonds; 2 oz butter. Divide the pastry into two pieces, and roll out each piece to a thin square. Mix the currants, peel, spices and almonds, and stir into the melted butter. Spread this filling evenly on to one piece of pastry to within one inch of the edge. Moisten the edge with water, and press on the second piece of pastry. Press the edges together well. With the back of a knife, mark the top of the pastry into two-inch squares without cutting through the filling. Bake at 425°F, 220°C, gas mark 7 for 25 minutes. Sprinkle with caster sugar and divide into small cakes where marked, while still warm.

MESS

Throughout the region from the coast through my own central Colne/Stour area to the extreme north-west frontier at Ashdon have come the mentions of MESS. The Ashdon one, for example, said mess was bread soaked in hot water with added salt and pepper. The word was widely used, however, for hundreds of years to cover various kinds of semi-liquid, pulpy foods, thick broths and concoctions. Milk sop was also called mess and the subject is further dealt with under SOPS and SOUP. Shakespeare uses the word but perhaps the best known is (as always) the Biblical reference, Esau's mess of pottage.

Onions

ONIONS

Today we normally restrict our raw onions to the Spring variety, though a large onion very thinly sliced makes a tomato salad exciting. The farmworker used to eat raw onions with his bread "to help get it down" and flavour it. Rider Haggard in his book 'Rural England', 1902, reports from Witham his meeting with John Lapwood. Lapwood told him that for months at a time he had existed upon nothing but a diet of bread and onions. He ate onions until they took the skin off the roof of his mouth and said that in his young days his wages as a horseman were nine shillings a week while during the Crimean war bread cost him one shilling a loaf. He grew his onions on his own patch. As we have already seen, butter or cheese could not always be afforded during hard times and Lapwood said that when there was butter or cheese in the house most of it went to his eight children.

When it comes to cooking onions the simplest ways may well be the best. BAKED ONIONS "Great Granny Nice of Gestingthorpe used to bake onions in their skins. She just put them on a baking tray in the oven for about two hours. Then she peeled them and served with cheese or butter."

Other vegetables like beetroot, swede and turnip are good baked. My lunch while writing this book has often consisted of a selection of root vegetables popped into the Aga oven. I was initiated into this practice by Peter Owen of Bulmer Tye whose culinary skills are only excelled by his woodworking ones.

From a 19th Century Coggeshall recipe book comes:

SALAD FOR COLD MEAT OR FOWL   Boil some Spanish onions, cut them up and mix the pieces with slices of raw tomatoes, pour oil and vinegar over the whole, and serve with cold meat.

Kathleen Barrell of Wivenhoe used to sing to me when preparing onions:

Oh, he's off his Spanish Onion, off his onion, off his onion, off his onion,
Round the room with the kitchen broom,
He's off his Spanish Onion.

She had been the contralto for the Chapel Concert Party and suggested that this vocal exercise prevented her eyes watering. Immersing onions before, during and after peeling in a bowl of water is a more reliable method. An old Victorian joke about workhouse masters admitted that they sometimes shed a tear for their inmates – but only when those inmates were peeling onions in the workhouse kitchen at the time. Onions were an ingredient of many of the boiled puddings that were eaten before the meat appeared on the table (if there was any meat to follow). The following recipe would feed two:

ONION PUDDING   Two middle sized onions, 4 oz of flour, 1 oz of suet (you can now buy vegetarian suet if you prefer it). Mix the flour and suet and add the chopped up onion, mixing it all to a puddingy consistency. Add a little salt. Tie the mixture in a pudding cloth and put it in a saucepan of boiling water. It will need at least an hour's boiling. Essex sometimes added a few lumps of bacon or streaky pork to this pudding. Just the job to keep out the cold.

My mother in law, Ethel, had a good reputation for PICKLED ONIONS. The usual recipe involves peeling small onions and soaking them in brine (wet brine: 2 oz salt to a pint of cold water) for at least 36 hours. After thorough rinsing and draining, the cold spiced vinegar is added. Standard pickling spice mixture is used, though my wife would insist that Juniper berries should be included because of a forebear who bore that interesting name. When Ethel had done the bottling, the results were hidden from her family until some months had passed. Commercial pickled onions sometimes served with pub ploughman's lunches do not taste as good. I think she added a teaspoon of sugar to the spiced vinegar, which was a level tablespoon of spice to a pint of vinegar and boiled together for 15 minutes.

In the 19th century wasp stings were rubbed with a raw onion and afterwards a slice was bound on. Margery Allingham said that awkward or expensive suggestions or remedies were termed "sarcastic" in Essex. The simplicity of the remedy above would have met with approval. "Fair jonnock" my mother might have said. The least sarcastic cure I have ever come across is for a belly ache – warm a large dinner plate and tie it on the affected part! Boiled onions were also put on the ear to treat earache. " I doubt that did na harm, do that did'n do na good".

An Essex woman looking back to her childhood in Finchingfield in the twenties said that, when she took her farmworker father's food to the fields, SPRING ONION SANDWICHES were a favourite. Try them. Chopped fine and used sparingly there is no danger of you blistering your mouth like Lapwood.

A final memory from one of my informants acts as our Onion Envoi: "When I was poorly I was allus put to bed with a belly full of onion gruel".

PIGS and PORK

To a Roast Pig

Rev. Charles Lesingham Smith, Rector of Little Canfield, 1839-1878 from 'Footprints on my Path of Life':

O Pig, or rather, little pork, once pig,
Smoking so daintily upon the table,
Making each gazer long that he were able,
To eat thee every limb, both small and big.
No more in squeaking flight, or grunting jig,
Thou runn'st about the straw yard, stye, or stable,
Nor bump'st thy little side against the gable;
Nor cock'st thy snout, a judge without a wig!
All other viands which I ever saw
Served up in silver, crockery ware, or tin,
Whether boil'd, roasted, bak'd, stew'd, fried or raw,
Compared with thee are worthless as a pin!
Sweet delicate meat ' crackling without a flaw!
What ho! a knife and fork! I must begin!

There is a caricature by Richard Newton entitled 'Which Way Shall I Turn Me?' It shows an 18th century parson sitting between a roast pig on a table and an attractive woman. Bearing this in mind and the fact that parsons' memoirs (especially the gouty Woodforde) are often greatly concerned with lavish meals, the poem above seemed appropriate to begin this section.

An Essex parson, William Harrison of Radwinter, wrote in 1587, "As for swine there is no place that hath greater store nor more wholesome in eating than are those here in England which nevertheless do never any good till they come to the table. Of these some we eat green for pork and other dried up into bacon to have it of more continuance". The story that no part of the pig was ever wasted is reinforced by his going on to say, "In some places women do scour and wet their clothes with pigs dung as others do with hemlocks and nettles but such is the savor of the clothes touched withal that I cannot abide to wear them on my body".

Before he came to live at Long Melford the poet Edmund Blunden wrote an often anthologised piece called 'The Poor Man's Pig'. It shows the cottager's pig released from the sty and with hungry hubbub begging crusts and orts from the cottage door. Barley was needed as well as orts and before we look at the importance of the backyard pig in the cottage economy it might be as well to say that not every poor countryman could afford to keep a pig and some were discouraged from doing so by their employers. Later, health regulations stopped them and I well remember one Finchingfield man's indignation about this when he invited me to consider the 'hygienic' conditions of intensive pig rearing which took the place of cottage pigs. 'Tulip' Rowe wrote that two-fifths of Bulmer's households kept a pig at the end of the 19th century.

Phil Rowe also of Bulmer, talking to me about the early years of our century said, "We had very good food. My dad had 13 shillings pay, a shilling more than his mates. He always had two pigs in the sty and as soon as one was fat that was put up the chimney for bacon, home cured (I can't even eat it now for indigestion). And we always had a big knob of fat pork with greens. There was mostly a local man, Dixey on the Tye, to kill the pigs, an ex-butcher. Course that was quite a pantomime to get a pan of water to scald it and scrape it. We kiddies used to watch the man scalding it to get all the bristles orf and then of course he hung it up and everything come out and we used to love to see the pluck. Whenever they killed a pig next door, everyone was the same, there was always someone killing a pig so you used to git pluck orf somebody or give it to somebody. We had better food. It was home made food and we could get 'em orf each other whenever we killed a pig".

Phil was thinking back to a period when agriculture was depressed. The Vicar's daughter at Benfleet, Miss Henderson, kept her diary from 1846 to 1872 which was one of the better periods in the 19th century for farming. She wrote, "I cannot bring myself to think the labourer's lot was so unhappy. Wages low but so were rents, tea and coffee dear but necessities cheap, their own grown vegetables, cured bacon (everyone kept one or two pigs), home-made bread from their own gleaned flour, fresh fish which could be bought for next to nothing".

For a long time the East Anglian equivalent to the fatted calf was fat pork with peas or greens. Charles Benham in one of his Essex Ballads of 1895, tells the story of the man who returns to his Essex family after being out foreign:

> He set there as happy as yer please,
> An' Missus laid the supper while he tork;
> A praphper set out, too, fat pork an' peas –
> 'Jim olluz was a mark,' she say, 'on pork.'

The little village butcher's shops, often the front room of a cottage, were frequently pork only establishments. One of my grandmothers used to say that she was off to buy a shiver of pork (pron. shivva). Claxton says that in Suffolk a shiver was a piece off the thick end of a fore leg of pork, usually salted and boiled. Moor for the 1820s in the same county says it was a piece or slice of anything. One of John Ray's Essex proverbs takes us back several centuries, "Tis safe taking a shive of a cut loaf".

I propose now to deal with the various products of the pig under separate headings; but having started with parsons in this section I finish with them. The corbel at end of a beam in the chancel of Finchingfield church represents the vicar with his little tithe pig by his side.

PORK CHEESE

In a Mary Mann short story a dying Norfolk woman says to her daughter, "What! Are you after making a pork-cheese? Lawk but that du smell good. I don't know how that is, but I hev had such a fancy for a piece o'pork since I was took ill". She was persuaded to take some and, needless to say, she got better.

The more widespread word for pork cheese is brawn. Harrison writing from Radwinter for England uses the word brawn. The use of the word cheese is ancient, however, and not just the usage of our local grandparents because there is a recipe in an 18th century Essex Still Room Book on "How to make a flesh cheese". In earlier centuries brawns seem to have been "made commonly from the fore part of a tame boar". More recently a hock and trotters provided the meat or sometimes a salted head. The basic method was to stew the meat till tender, then strain off the stock which was boiled down and poured over the cut-up seasoned meat, put in a mould or moulds and turned out when cold.

I have been given a number of recipes from all over our region. Some Cambridgeshire and Essex ones used hocks only, some from Suffolk and Essex used only trotters and others used only meat from the head. Sage, grown outside the back door, was the most favoured herb for flavouring and the spices included nutmeg, cloves, mace and peppercorns. Several informants have told me that when pork cheese was around the head of the household had it for breakfast.

The recipe comes from Eastern Essex.

Wash a pig's head in salt water and rub it with salt and brown sugar. Rub in fresh salt for three days. Then cover with cold water and stew it with bay leaves and an onion stuck with cloves. When the meat is tender take it off the bones, cut it up and add spice, sage and seasoning. The tongue should be skinned and used. The basin (s) should be filled and some of the liquid added. Turn it out when cold.

CHITTERLINGS

These were the cleaned intestines of the pig used in various ways. Mrs Osmond mentions them as a Suffolk favourite in 1903 when made into pies. For pies or turnovers, you need to simmer the chitterlings till tender, chop them and add chopped apple and some currants, sweeten and season before using the mixture. Hilary, my wife, made some turnovers for an "OLD FOOD" occasion; but again, when people found out what was in them, some were dismayed.

Chitterlings were often given away. One family, which regularly killed a pig in the autumn, remembered how a neighbour used to hang about watching until he came out with "Who's hevving the guts?"

SCRAPS, SCRITS and SCRITTENY

A Polstead woman in her eighties remembered, "The butcher always killed his pigs on Mondays, and on Tuesdays, in his shop, were lovely sausages, pork cheeses and a big dish of scraps. On Tuesday, as a treat, mother would send one of us for a pennyworth of scraps for our tea. We ate them with salt and bread. They were the remains of all the pork fat that the butcher had tried down to get his lard". In Essex these scraps were more often called scrips, scrits or scritlings. And a kind of cake known as scritteny was made out of flour, scrits and skim.

Scritteny was particularly favoured in the Braintree area. Mrs L. R. Headly of Rayleigh sent a similar recipe to 'Essex Countryside.'. It consisted of flour, scraps, nutmeg, bicarb, currants, sugar and milk to mix. It is obviously a rather better version of scritteny. Major Moor, whose book called Suffolk Words & Phrases (1823) must be one of the most readable books on dialect ever devised, finished his mention of scraps with "some gross feeding persons like these pieces fried". A Finchingfield woman, talking to me about the 1920s, remembered "fritters" which turned out to be pork fat fried, so there were some gross feeders in Essex as well.

FROLICS and RUNTS

At fetes and frolics one could bowl for a pig or there was the time-honoured pastime of competing to catch a pig by its tail which had been well greased. One East Anglian memory was of women, several of them buxom bonkers, having a go and the fascination of watching the slippery appendage slide through their fingers until a very fat woman finally fell on it and won.

There are many stories of women who became very good at mothering the little runts who were the weak ones in the litter and not likely to survive without being hand reared with a bottle. When bringing up these tiny piglets some of these foster mothers became understandably very fond of them. Perhaps the most extraordinary example of this was printed in the Halstead Gazette for 12th December 1901. A father and daughter were before the Petty Sessions court. A sanitary inspector said in evidence that (on information) he visited the house and found a pig lying between sheets on a feather bed. The daughter said she had had it for four years and had brought it up. It was house trained and ate at their table. She added that " it behaved in many respects like a Christian". The sad end of the story was that they were ordered to provide a suitable place for the pig, outside the house.

Nazeing, on the other side of Essex, provided another example of this pig in the family situation. The Nazeing Pig was the pet of a woman who lived there in the 1890s. Visitors went to see it in "a lovely bed with white sheets all lace edged".

In our own century an Essex school caretaker had brought up a number of runts for her pig keeping brothers. One day a man who was very good with clocks, agreed to go to her cottage to adjust her wall clock." You'll hev to stand on the sofa to get to it," she said to him. " I reckon I shall find that difficult," he said because the old horse hair sofa was almost entirely covered, indeed in places overlapped, by a large sleeping pig.

"Git orf dew," she said, giving it a shove. When the job was finished and the "clock tickler" was thanked, he saw, out of the corner of his eye as he went out, that the pig was being helped back up again.

I came across references at Gt Welnetham and Hadleigh to the old Suffolk tradition that elder sisters should dance in a hog's trough if the youngest sister married before them. Could this have anything to do with an Essex Countryside reprint of an 1814 item from a column of births, deaths and marriages – "At Broomfield, Mrs Harris suffered in the hogtub".

PORRIDGE

When John Castle of Coggeshall went into the workhouse in 1837 he was given "seven ounces of bread and about one pint of skilley for breakfast". He details his workhouse diet in his diary; and surviving diet boards and sheets give us confirmation of the new Union workhouse fare at this time. You will not be surprised to learn that bread made up the greater part of the paupers' diet. Skilley was a very thin type of oatmeal porridge or gruel. It amuses me to recollect that this was the word for porridge when I was at college in 1943, as well as being an army term. Come to think of it the college breakfast cook was a First World War veteran who was also our Home Guard sergeant. When we went on an exercise he would encourage us beforehand by saying "Them men who deserves medals will get medals". I wondered if they would be given for bravery in the field or for eating his skilly.

I asked a Senior Citizens' Group in Halstead what they usually had for breakfast when they were young. More than half said it was bread in some form and most of the rest said porridge. The bread eaters had dripping or butter or jam or something else to help get it down. A few mentioned milk sops or water mess (q.v.) and quite a number had the bread fried. Two had egg and bacon on Sundays and one man maintained stoutly, despite his companions' amusement, that rabbit pie was his breakfast staple.

The many other older country dwellers that I have talked to or recorded have provided ample confirmation that it was usually bread for breakfast, but the younger my informants the more likely porridge is to be mentioned.

In 1913 the Rowntree Survey gives an Essex labourer's diet for a typical week. For breakfast, bread and butter, toast and porridge are the three variants. For his dinner his wife rang the changes on these daily menus: day 1, suet pudding; day 2, potatoes and apple pudding; day 3, dumplings and vegetables; day 4, dripping and potatoes; day 5, soup, potatoes, bread; day 6, soup, dumplings, potatoes. Sunday tended to be the one day when there might be a bit of meat in the pudding. The labourer's tea was bread with either butter or sugar. He was the only member of the family who got supper and that was bread again with a little cheese or beetroot.

RECIPE   Stir a $1/4$ lb of oatmeal into a quart of boiling water with a little salt in it, boil gently for half an hour, stirring occasionally to prevent it sticking to the pan (you hope). Alternatively get yourself a double saucepan.

Gruel gets a mention under invalid food.

Potatoes

POTATOES

Big gardens for vegetable growing were common in the countryside. Sometimes the men also had an allotment and there were allotments in towns, as well, of course. "They were big gardens often or a dozen rod. They used to dig 'em at night after tea". Long hours of work on the land meant that allotments sometimes had to be dug by moonlight. "Nowadays they wouldn't even dig 'em in the day time, would they?" said Ernie Pilgrim of Wickham St Paul. An Edwardian horseman's wife from Rivenhall remembered that the farm had "a field of potatoes from which each worker was allowed to dig one row for his family's use".

Bulmer Tye's large waste or common was enclosed to make allotments in 1840; and, during the 19th century in bad years when the potato crop was poor, Bulmer asked no rent for those allotments. The little strips of garden near the farm cottages were labelled on the 19th century maps as potato gardens. Both these facts make it quite clear what the main crop was and the importance of potatoes in the diet. They were mostly boiled. Jack Allen of Bardfield said "Our potatoes in the net didn't go to mash". This refers to the practice of separating the potatoes in a net from the other food cooking in the big black boiling pan on the fire. Phil Rowe of Bulmer said that his father made the nets specially for this purpose. One big family I knew in the 1960s always went to school on a breakfast of fried potatoes. The mother boiled enough the day before to fry up a huge pan of them with lard in the mornings.

It is interesting to see that the jacket potato today seems to be making a dent in the popularity of chips. Suffolk liked a bait o' taters and was known to call the mouth a tater trap. An Essex boy I taught 20 years ago who used this word tater, had problems when he tried to spell it in a more high falutin way:

Creative Writing

The children are creating. Nothing unusual about that you will say. Shirley wants to talk about her ideas; very persuasively she tells Lucy all about them, quietly, but with extravagant gestures and quiet eyes. A communicator? Yes, but there won't be much on the paper at the end of the lesson.

Lucy (if she gets a chance) will work very slowly, take a long time to think it out, but could do best of all.

Nicholas is about to fall off his chair.

Glen has been out to me twice to show me his first two lines.

Shirley is still talking.

There's some very frenzied rubbing out going on over there. Self doubt no doubt. Erasure to ensure composure.

Graham has come out for a word to be spelled.

"Couldn't you find it in the dictionary?"

"Ass not there!"

"What word is it?"

"Bertater."

"Try P, Graham, poe-tay- toe not bert-hate-o."

Shirley is writing now.

Alison has written most eloquently of her inability to write anything.

Later, when I read them through, I can hear them again, though they have long since gone home. As I read, their voices read their efforts to me. Their characters, their personalities, even the ink smudge where Nicholas's chair finally did fall over, are all there in their work. And Graham has spelt potatoes sensibly, economically, "taters." I wonder whether to cross this out and write instead in the margin, "This is ollus spelled 'SPUD' ".

Potatoes are undoubtedly tasty, however cooked, and satisfyingly filling. James Blyth's excellent East Anglian stories, which have been discovered for us by E. A. Goodwyn, include one called 'The Poor Man's Potato'. In the early Edwardian years the sister of the lord of the village, has, she assures her Colonel brother, been insulted by a labourer. Accused of this the offender said, "I niver said narthen. She come on the allotment, a fussin' about, like she allust dew. 'My good man' she say ' an what's the name o' the taters yewr'e a settin?' Soo I tode har and she let out a screech and went toddlin' off. She's wholly a rum egg". Asked, of course, what the name of the potato variety was by the Colonel, he used the name by which the variety, 'Imperator', was always known in the village – Gut-busters. "I niver knowed no other name for 'em as trew as I stand here." In the story he is duly turned out of his cottage by his landlord and imperator.

Just as East Anglians took their local words and their witchcraft with them to America, so I think dishes like 'Hash-Brown Potatoes' (Time Life's 'Vegetables') may have found their way to us across the Atlantic. I think my favourite way with potatoes is to slice them and some onions thinly, place them in layers in a dish, add stock, or milk or sauce and bake slowly in the oven. But then what about my Grandfather's first digging of new potatoes served without embellishments of any kind?

PUDDINGS

In mediaeval times one Abbess of the great abbey of Barking in Essex had her own separate kitchen with its cooks and "pudding wife". A very old ballad sung at Harvest Homes in Norfolk reinforces the region's liking for pudding:

> King Arthur was a prudent king, a prudent king, a prudent king
> King Arthur was a prudent king.
> He bought five sacks o' barley meal to make a large pudding.
> And a large pudden it was indeed and well stuffed with plums
> With great big jobs of suet in as big as my two thumbs.

It was indeed prudent to provide plenty of nourishing and cheap suet pudding to fill your family.

Ruth Whybrow (born 1897) of Nayland and Halstead, said, "Mother was very good at making suet puddings. She would send one of us to the butchers for a pennyworth of beef suet. We only had meat and veg. for dinner once a week on Sunday. All the week it was two slices of suet pudding and then back to school. Mother varied the puddings which were cooked in a cloth in a great big iron sauce-pan. Sometimes she would make a plain suet and we would have brown sugar on it. Sometimes we would have a currant or a raisin or an apple one. On special occasions we had one of her meat puddings but that was very rare".

Chambers Encyclopedia for 1865 has, "Puddings are either made of dough simply boiled in a cloth or basin or they may be made of a batter and poured into the pudding cloth and boiled or into a dish and baked (see section on batter). It is common to make puddings by rolling out dough or paste into large flat sheets and enclosing the fruit or meat entirely in them and then tying them up in the pudding cloth and boiling them".

Mim Frost of Belchamp Otten says, "My grandmother used to make them all individual puddings, one for each of the men and have them all boiling in the copper in the outhouse with their names written on the cloths. They were 11 in family and with them coming in at different times, she would take out each man his own pudding. She used old sheet as her pudding cloths. On the suet puddings they might have a bit of gravy left over from the Sunday meat, or a little butter, or sugar or syrup".

Bessie Walford of Little Maplestead said that "cloth puddings" began to be thought of as less respectable than those cooked in a basin; but she and her husband, Reg, confirmed that butter, gravy, syrup, treacle or sugar were served with the suet pudding.

Jack Allen of Bardfield said that in the evenings they had suet puddings in a round linen cloth, boiled for about an hour, sometimes with vegetables and potatoes. "There were no ovens – all cooked on the fire in a big boiler".

One of my Finchingfield contributors said, "Me mother had seven of us and she could make a meal out of nothing. Occasionally she would get six pennyworth of meat pieces for a pudding cooked in a big old boiler on the fire". When there was a bit of meat, bacon and onion pudding was an Essex favourite. Pork and onion were also used in the Clanger and it is this type of pudding that I turn to next.

The clanger was savoury at one end and sweet on the other. You roll out a stiff crust of self raising flour and beef suet and fill one half with, say, streaky pork and onion and the other half with fruit or jam. Roll it up and, to stop the contents mixing, tie it in the centre. Flour well and put it in the cloth. Steam it for $1\frac{1}{2}$ hr. Bedfordshire Clangers were described as long roll puddings with meat at one end and jam at the other. Cambridgeshire went in for Onion Clangers with meat when available. In 1985 Albert Hare (then 79 years) contributed a piece to a recipe book published by my WEA class at Great Oakley. He said that his mother invented the Pitsea Clanger which "within several years became famous" in that part of Essex. It was a long pudding wrapped in muslin or an old stocking and boiled for 12 hours. "The skill was in the contents which were divided into sealed compartments as per rough sketch."

Meat	Spuds	Cabbage	Yorkshire pudding	Jelly gravy	Apples	Thick custard	Jam

"Sadly with modern methods today the Pitsea Clanger has long been forgotten," added Mr. Hare.

That ought to be the last word on puddens but it might be worth recording that long church sermons in East Anglia were known as pudden-spilers and that when an Essex dad removed the stocking or bandages from the pudding prior to cutting it up for serving to the family he had been known to say, "Now, who's for a slice of granny's leg ?"

Having started our account of puddings in a great mediaeval institution, Barking Abbey, I finish it in a smaller one, the Wivenhoe Village Workhouse. The overseers' accounts provide these two entries:

1799 paid for a peice of cloth for four pudden Bags for the Workhouse 9d.

1806 the new Master and wife (under Article 7) to allow three Hot Dinners per week such as good wholesom puddings.

BLACK PUDDINGS

These were popular locally as well as in the North. A Finchingfield man born in 1861 remembered being sent to the butcher to fetch home free blood and a pennyworth of suet for black puddings for the family. Mediaeval artists showed the making of these puddings in pans or skins at the time of the winter pig killings.

Roots

ROOTS

SWEDES

An Earls Colne farmer told me, after I had spoken at a Halstead Rotarians lunch, that a few swedes were sown with the mangolds. When harvested they were all clamped together so that as the mangolds were gradually taken out for animal feed a few swedes would gradually become available for the house. The same thing went on in Suffolk. George Hoggart said, "The lads used to put a packet of swedes in with the mangolds and these were clamped together to provide the lads with food".

A good dollop of swede is a very "tasty conflaption" if mashed with a little butter. They can also be cut into slices and boiled in salted water. When the slices were cooked a little butter or dripping, if either was available, was added to them just before serving.

A Suffolk railwayman's daughter from Elmsett said of the early 1900s "Our dinners were very scanty. I have known the time when all we had was swedes". The five daughters all went into service, one son became a driver, one went into the army and one died.

CARROTS

In the early 19th Century Edward Moor from Suffolk said that roots which were a bit dry or shrivelled were called CLUNG but that carrots were better for horses like this than too RESH. Certainly a not too seriously shrivelled root will come up again if soaked before being cooked. I prefer my carrots raw to cooked. Modern interest in crudités, dips and soaking grated carrot in fruit juice has helped to keep them popular in the raw state; but where would boiled salt beef be without the carrots?

PARSNIPS

A bait of parsnips is a welcome addition to a meal. Like carrots they make good soup but many feel that they are best baked plain in the oven or roasted with a little fat or cooked in the meat tray. My maternal grandfather, postman Cook, grew very good parsnips in his large Wivenhoe garden. He dusted a little soot round when storing them and he relished them with his Sunday meat.

Parsnips mashed with a little butter and topped with breadcrumbs look good and a few chopped nuts, seeds or pine kernels make it a grand dish. Parsnips are good in soufflés too if you really want to go up market.

TURNIPS

Moor gives us the pleasing phrase, "Turnip is sarce to bield beef". Sarce or saace (rhyming with brass) was the Suffolk for sauce and it was used to describe vegetables as accompaniments to dishes. Turnips are not so widely eaten today,

I suppose, more often being used for soup. Taken to feed hungry bellies, they have often featured in the annals of the poor.

In this connection the records of Ridgewell Congregational Church give us a moving glimpse of Essex chapel discipline for 1837. Daniel Daynes was accused of pulling six turnips, from the field where he was working with his mate, for breakfast. He had done it without thinking but repented of his sin so the church took no other action except to suggest that he refrain from attendance at Communion till after the next Ordinance Day.

When mashing turnips a local recipe book suggests putting a couple of boiled potatoes through a sieve with the boiled turnips, seasoning with salt and pepper and adding a little milk. A potato masher is just as effective as sieving.

"DO PEAS TRY AND TURNIP TO THYME FOR THE BEANFEAST" ran a Victorian invitation card which I was shown in an Essex village. With that sense of humour it could only be a Victorian one. The card manufacturers of the period seem to have had their fingers on the public pulse and to have been well rooted in the popular taste of the day.

Turnips turn up finally in two ways. First as the subject of a one time very popular song much in favour at rural entertainments:

Twas on a jolly summers morn, the twenty first of May
Giles Scroggins took his turmut hoe with which he trudged away

runs the verse and the refrain has:

For the fly, the fly, the fly is on the turmut
And its all my eye for we to try to keep fly off the turmut

That very gallant gentleman, Captain Oates, who on Scott's Antarctic expedition stumbled into the blizzard to save his companions, was the son of the Squire of Gestingthorpe. As a boy interested in animals, he spent many hours on the estate watching the horsemen and farmworkers and listening to them. When he and his companions spent months in their huts waiting for the weather to improve before the attempt on the South Pole could start, they whiled away the time with songs and stories to entertain each other. You have already guessed which was the favourite song in Oates' repertoire and it doesn't require much imagination to guess where he heard

The song concludes:

Now all you jolly farming lads as bides at home so warm
I now concludes my ditty with wishing you no harm.
For the fly, the fly, the fly is on the turmut
And it's all my eye for we to try to keep fly off the turmut.

I find it satisfying that Oates, when out abroad, remembered his roots.

Salads

SALADS

A popular song for delivery at Harvest Homes and village concerts with a certain nudging emphasis was:

Come to tea on Sunday night – winkles and water cresses
A nice little girl to sit on your knee – winkles and water cresses.
Pa's gone out, Ma's not in, Cook she's gone to her niece's.
There's only the parrot and he won't talk – winkles and water cresses.

That Sunday tea was the time for water cress is confirmed by Old Philip Rowe of Bulmer writing in the late 1920s and looking back to the last century. "We had suppers for we never said tea only on a Sunday when we had a good cooked dinner with a bit of meat, got a good fill, the only time perhaps we all had our dinner together – and a good dinner at that – a good way to know a Sunday. On Sunday then we called tea, 'tea' for we wanted little else unless celery or water cress (or other salad we liked) to push a little bit of bread and butter down. Not so when I had been using a scythe all day, then walked two or three miles to get home, we wanted a supper then. Not Tea."

Water cress, locally collected in streams and ponds, is mentioned by several older East Anglians, but isn't Philip Rowe's sorting out of the names of meals entirely convincing? Definitely the last word on the subject. An Ilford man remembered that among the street callers was the water cress man who came round on Sunday afternoons selling a handful.

When William Scrivener, cook to the Corporation of Kings Lynn, died, this verse was written, "Modern squeamish stomachs and ye curious palates / You've lost your dainty dishes and your salades / Mourn for yourselves, but not for him i' th' least / He's gone to taste of a more Heav'nly feast".

To go with a Corporation cook we need something special. The Suffolk Salad given by Florence White therefore follows:

SUFFOLK SALAD Fill a salad bowl from half to three parts full with very tender lettuces shred small, minced lean of ham, and hard boiled eggs or their yolks only, also minced, placed in alternate layers, dress the mixture with English salad sauce, but do not pour it into the bowl until the instant of serving. The eggs may be sliced instead of being minced.

Doesn't that sound excellent ? Come to think of it, my mother's egg salad was rather like it. I used to admire her skill at slicing the hard boiled eggs before she bought a little string instrument for doing the job. Decorating salads and trifles was of a somewhat competitive nature among my female elders.

SAUSAGES

Tom Hood, the Victorian poet, lived at Epping at one time. In his "The Epping Hunt" (1829) we find this:

Epping for butter justly famed
And pork in sausage pop't
Where winter time or summer time
Pig's flesh is always chop't.

The recipe collected by Florence White for Epping sausages bears almost the same date, 1826.

SKINLESS EPPING SAUSAGES   Young pork 3 lb, beef suet 3 lb, sage leaves, thyme, savory and marjoram, half a lemon, nutmeg, pepper & salt and as much egg as will make it smooth. Fry in clarified fat or grill.

Similar recipes are around for Suffolk. A Cambridgeshire version mixes equal quantities of pork and bacon with smaller amounts of beef and veal, twice as much of the former as of the latter.

Phil Rowe of Bulmer told me how to make sausages: "You get the ropes from the pig and clean 'em. You get odd bits of meat and bread all mixed up and you poke it through a funnel with the ropes fixed on it. Tha's rough and ready but good eating, better'n you can git now, I can tell you. We had better food. It was home made food and we could get meat orf each other whenever we killed a pig".

I can remember my grandfathers and other elders frequently complaining that sausages were not what they were.

"Bags of mystery" was the phrase. It certainly isn't easy to get a decent sausage today. There was no mystery about one of their ingredients. They contained a great deal of what is considered today to be unhealthy – fat. The Irish poet, W. R. Rodgers, who lived in the area and listened to its inhabitants, offered a different explanation of the unsatisfactory nature of the modern sausage by quoting an Essex man: "It's all those Conservatives they put in them nowadays".

Very much earlier England made sausage which we would think of today as continental. Sir Hugh Plat in 1609 gives the formula for this splendid sawsedge or polony.

POLONIAN SAWSEDGE   Pork chopped fine, with red sage, season with ginger & pepper and put it into a great sheepes gut. Soak three nights in brine, then boile it and hang it up in a chimney where fire is usually kept and these sawsedges will last one whole year. They are good for sallades or to make one relish a cup of wine.

The 19th and early 20th century village pork butchers often had a fine reputation. C. Henry Warren, who lived at Finchingfield, beautifully describes the products of one of them:

" For miles around Mr. Wright was famed for his sausages. People speak of them even today with a delight and a longing that suggest their savour still lingers on the palate. His pork cheeses were a delicacy enjoyed far beyond his parish; but his proper pride was in his sausages. I verily believe he would think it neither immodest nor irreligious if the fact should be commemorated on his tombstone".

I made the pilgrimage to Finchingfield churchyard to see if the inscription had, in fact, been placed; but couldn't find it. Wasn't his lady lucky, though ? She found her Mr. Wright (butchers have such killing ways, you know) – and an artist in bangers into the bargain.

We continue this symposium on the sausage by returning to Phil Rowe. I tape recorded him in the cottage which his builder nephew Peter has now so interestingly restored, and named in his memory. Philip had lived through the hungry agricultural depressions since 1880, but had in more recent times been able to enjoy a sausage for breakfast sometimes. He said:

"I've always bin a heavy eater but not an expensive eater. Now, I have one sausage for breakfast and I get three or four slices of bread and butter down with that, but I don't want two. Chaps today they want two sausages and a hegg as well".

As he delivered himself of these sentiments I could see a question formulating itself and, with the courtesy of the countryman, he looked across at me and quickly added, "Then perhaps you like two sausages too. You see there's a lot of difference with the way some people live".

In fact I was a one sausage man. Now I am a no sausage man except when I stay in hotels and think I may as well have my fill of the paid-for traditional English breakfast. I can't say the modern hotel sausage is anything to write home about; but my mother's beef and bacon sausage – that was a very different matter. It is curious that she and her mother both firmly rejected the idea of buying beef sausages from the butcher. It had to be pork. Beef ones were barely respectable. However their Beef and Bacon Roll (as they called it to distinguish it from sausages with skins) was a legitimate reason for culinary pride. The preparation and the cooking always began to make my mouth water as a child because I looked ahead to a succession of delicious cold slices.

EDITH'S BEEF AND BACON SAUSAGE   1 lb of lean beef¹/₂ lb of fat bacon, 2 cups of bread crumbs, 1 egg, parsley, seasoning and a little mushroom ketchup or Worcester sauce

First mince meats finely, then add breadcrumbs and seasoning, mixing it together with a beaten egg. Shape it into a roll and either boil in a floured cloth for a couple of hours or cook it in a steamer. Eat hot or cold. It was a Christmas time favourite for my Wivenhoe family; but, of course, eats well at any time of year. There are Essex recipes for a similar dish made with mutton and bacon.

SHRIMPS

I used to be astonished by the rapidity with which the older generations of my family could demolish a bowl of shrimps. I quite liked them as a child but my slow struggles with head, tail and armour plated slides meant that I managed one to my grandparents ten. A. E. Copping's Gotty from Thameside, Essex found "the little pink uns sweeter" but "the brown uns thought more of, seein as they're bigger".

The catchers boiled them on board boat on the way back and sometimes did the selling themselves. I remember the cry of the Green family of Wivenhoe was "Shrimp-O" as they came through the village. Other sellers took up a pitch in the towns and a dwarf shrimp seller was often to be seen at Scheregate steps in Colchester. A Suffolk woman's cry was "Fresh boiled shrimps sold by the catcher!"

Brown bread and butter goes well with shrimps; but they are not as plentiful today as they were when Sabine Baring Gould, the parson at Mersea, used to sit and share a pail of them with the Bakers who lived in an old boat there in the 1870s.

Seaside outings were not complete without the shrimp tea. Gestingthorpe choir in the 1890s, according to its vicar, went to Messrs Day's establishment in Clacton for theirs. The East coast knew about shrimps. Gestingthorpe was not enthusiastic about the peas, however, provided in some of the other catering establishments – "they had reached the sere and yellow".

Oh, the smell of shrimps, crabs, seaweed, steam trains and rain damped clothing! What bliss it was to go on an excursion to the sea. Harwich shrimps were highly regarded; and, because on your trip "it had to be shrimps for tea, Maldon was not Maldon without them.".

The fresh ones available from the fishmongers today tend to be a bit limp. Frozen and potted ones taste O.K. however and today's passion for expensive imported prawns can be circumvented by using a few shrimps in fish recipes. I don't understand the current obsession with prawns.

Gotty should be allowed the last word from Leigh: "London flies to big winkles same as it does to big shrimps but our little uns are wonderful sweet".

SOPS

Pieces of bread soaked in something liquid (hot water, milk, soup, gravy) have formed one of the most universally occurring meals from time immemorial.

Skimmed milk sops seem to have been more frequently eaten at breakfast time in our region than anything else at the turn of the century. An Earls Colne farmer told me that his grandmother was very fond of and swore by milk sops. During the war time air raid warnings the family took up their various appointed safe places in the farm house. His place as a child was with his grandmother in the cupboard under the stairs. If 9 p.m. came and they were incarcerated there, grandma still had to have her nightly sops. He said that he still disliked warm milk as a result of this experience and can still remember his discomfort because of the smell of the milk on the sops as she noisily imbibed in very close proximity to him.

Ernie Pilgrim of Wickham St Paul got the skimmed milk from Bullocks Hole Farm for his mother. "Boy, that was skimmed then – you could read the paper through it." Kate Rose (born 1882 in Polstead) said that her father always had bread and milk for breakfast: "I used to have to walk two miles to fetch the milk for breakfast. Then I did another two miles to walk to school". Ruth Whybrow adds her confirmation: "When we had bread and milk for breakfast I used to go to a farm for the milk at 7 a.m. in the morning. The can handle we carried used to nearly freeze to our fingers as we had no gloves".

Andrew Phillips, who has done much interesting research on the 19th century health of Colchester, quotes the Medical Officer of Health for the 1880s. He cites neglected dustbins and carelessness about infant feeding bottles (breast feeding was O.K.) which caused much diarrhoea and death. Cows milk was often adulterated and contaminated and when opium products failed to silence the babies, a lump of bread was administered soaked in a sugary mess of water and condensed milk for days on end and "left on the fire hob in a cup seldom or never changed or cleansed, whence the sooty mass is heaped into the infants mouth".

Tinned sweetened condensed milk became cheap and was widely used. Two of my informants have memories of secretly trying to eat a whole tin of condensed milk when they were children and regretting the attempt.

Lots of farm workers also went to work on KETTLE SOPS. This was bread broken up in lumps with boiling water poured on. Pepper and salt flavoured it and sometimes a little dripping. It tastes better than it sounds.

Bill Argent (born 1901), of Great Maplestead, called these hot water sops WATER MESS It was, he said, bread broken up, hot water added and a little butter.

Essex advice about eating sops in the 17th century was, "Be cautious and not over forward in dipping or sopping in the dish; and have a care of letting fall anything you are about to eat between the plate and your mouth". Had they known of it, his female relations would have liked to draw my paternal grandfather's attention to this advice. He liked to sop biscuits in his tea and pieces of bread in his boiled egg. If there was egg on his waistcoat when he came to visit us, my mother would sweetly ask, "What did you have for breakfast, father ?" His reply was "bloaters", regardless. On one such occasion I actually saw him print with an indelible pencil the words "red herrings" across the editorial of the newspaper, which my mother had spread on the kitchen table for her cooking, while he gave his answer.

The best sops were those made by dipping a piece of bread in the latch pan which was to put to catch the drippings of fat and juices that came out of the meat when it was cooking in front of the fire on a jack or spit. A very Senior Citizen of Halstead told me in 1988 that nothing could surpass these sops for flavour.

Raymond Lamont-Brown tells us that William Symons of Norfolk gave instructions for an iron dish to be fixed to his gravestone.

> Here lies my corpse, who was the man
> That loved a sop in the dripping pan;
> But now, believe me, I am dead.
> See how the pan stands at my head.
> Still for the sops till the last, I cried;
> But could not eat, and so I died.
> My neighbours, they perhaps will laugh
> When they do read my epitaph.

SOUP

It is right that sops and soup should find themselves together in this book because they come from the same root. La soupe in French still means sop or a soaked slice of bread. To link sops and soup we can quote John Gay of Beggar's Opera fame. His Marian feeds her man:

Strait on the Fire the sooty Pot I placed
To warm thy Broth I burnt my Hands for Haste.
When hungry thou stoodst staring like an Oaf
I sliced the luncheon from the Barley-Loaf.
With crumbled Bread I thickened well thy Mess.
Ah, love more, or love thy Pottage less.

Philip "Tulip" Rowe's father was born in 1842 and was a horseman. Tulip, of Bulmer, wrote, "He used to go early between 4 and 5 o'clock in summer. He did not have a lot of time to have anything before he went so my mother used to make him a can of tea, coffee or sometimes it would be a can of PEA SOUP [can to carry it in NOT the sort you use a can opener on!]. I had to take it to him on my way to school".

Mrs Ida Bird, born 1895, of Wickham St. Paul told me that as children (nine in family) they would be sent to school in cold weather on pea soup for breakfast. "Three mornings a week we went to school on a mess of pease soup made in a big boiler with bone stock." Notice she uses the same word, mess, as John Gay's Marian (c. 1728).

PEA SOUP   Soak and drain 12 oz of split peas beforehand. Then put the peas into 2 pints of water, bring to the boil, skim and cook slowly. Chop an onion and a carrot and soften them in ¹/₂ oz of dripping or butter. Add some herbs and a bay leaf. This should be added to the peas cooking in water and stock and cooked for at least an hour until the peas are soft. About a teaspoon of salt was cooked in with this and traditionally a little sugar was added. Either sieve, mouli or use the electric blender for the soup when it is ready. Some leek or spinach can be used to advantage with the onion and carrot. Serve bread with it or break some old bread up in it if you want your mess or pottage to be authentically filling.

Reasonably young and green pea pods make an excellent stock. Cook them with an onion and some bay leaves and then use the liquid to make your split or dried pea soup. 19th century Norfolk was fond of Carrot Soup. Start with a beef or mutton bone stock. Then put in your carrots which you have chopped up and cook till tender. Their soup was sieved. The electric blender is certainly a great boon to us today. Add a little pepper and warm it up again before serving. This like some other soups can taste better when it is reheated the following day. Some soups seem to taste better after freezing. No doubt the flavours of the ingredients have longer to mingle.

One of my favourites among these thick nourishing soups is Lovage and Potato.

ESSEX LOVAGE & POTATO SOUP   Take an onion or leek and a carrot or turnip (with, if available, some outside celery stalk), chop them and sweat them   for a while in a little butter or dripping or oil. Chop up a generous quantity of lovage and the raw or cooked potato. Boil all ingredients in some stock or water with a little seasoning and then simmer till cooked. Put in the blender, reheat and taste for seasoning. Lovage is a herb which grows very large and makes a fine plant for the corner of your garden or the back of a border. Its flavour combines well with the potato. Its early spring growth is the best.

Recipes are a bit pointless for soups as essentially they should be made from whatever ingredients are available, fresh or left over. Herbs and onion are in many of them; but, basically, they consist of a little of this and plenty of that. Mushroom and walnut ketchups, yeast extract and dried brewers yeast powder are useful for flavouring; and potatoes, flour and pulses for thickening. Meat, fish and vegetable stocks are essential for some; but some "Spring" soups neither need them nor are improved by them. Parsnips and pumpkins were East Anglian favourites as soups.

Florence White's "Good Things in England" was first published in 1932 and it *is* full of good things. She was a founder of the English Folk Cookery Association and that book and its follower are full of regional dishes. It was in her book that I first met the recipes of Mary Eaton of Bungay in Suffolk dating from 1823.

SUFFOLK SPRING SOUP Ingredients: Green peas 1 pint; chervil; purslain; lettuce; sorrel; parsley; onions 3 or 4; butter about 1 oz.; warm water; yolks of eggs 3; a gill of good milk; pepper; salt. Method: Put the peas with the vegetables and herbs (chopped up) in a stewpan with the butter. 2. Shake them over the fire for a few minutes. 3. Add warm water in proportion to the vegetables and stew till they are well covered. 4. Strain off the soup and pass the vegetables through a sieve. 5. Heat the pulp with three parts of the soup. 6. Mix the remainder with 3 yolks of eggs, a gill of milk and the rest of the soup and thicken it over the fire. 7. When ready to serve add it to the soup. 8. Heat the soup and thickening together and season to taste.

Mary Eaton's stock used lean beef and gammon stewed with carrots, onions and celery, which we might find expensive today, but she suggested boiling it only until the meat was tender and then using the beef and bacon to make a meat loaf or potted meat.

That previously mentioned 17th century Essex housewife had advice for soup eaters, "If your pottage be so hot your mouth cannot endure it, have patience till it be of a fit coolness: for it is very unseemly to blow it in your spoon or otherwise".

Angela Green's exemplary researched book on Ashdon in Essex, tells us that in the early 14th century a tenant of the Lord of the Manor there, provided the latter with men to work his harvest. The manor provided the workers with food including wheaten loaves and cabbage broth. This is a translation of "potag de choleas". Let's hope they enjoyed their mess of pottage.

Sprats

SPRATS

John Ray gives, as one of his 17th century sayings, "The Weavers beef of Colchester" – and their beef was sprats. One of his proverbs was "A Scot and a Yarmouth Herring go half the world over". I have already devoted a section to herrings but sprats are an equally important subject for regional social history. On 17th December 1775 the Wivenhoe parish clerk was paid 2d for removing sprats out of the churchyard. Across the river at Rowhedge the very first Sunday School class at the Mariners' Chapel was held up while a strong odour was located. The smell came from the scholars pockets which were found to contain sprats. The schoolmistress at Gestingthorpe in 1896 asked her charges to write essays on "How I should spend five shillings". One Gestingthorpe schoolboy's effort reached the pages of the Parish Magazine and it is a fascinating document:

"I should buy some shop things. I will buy a pair of braces, a straw hat, a pair of slippers for the baby, 3 herrings, 12 white herrings and 24 sprats. Then I will go to a chemist shop and buy a scent bottle and twopenny worth of fisic".

It will not surprise you that, given riches, he was going to spend some of them on filling his own stomach; but you may be a little surprised at his choice of food. It is eloquent testimony to the fact that, when country people got a change of diet, it was herrings and sprats that provided the change from bread, puddings and potatoes.

Sir John Martin Harvey, the Edwardian actor, spent much of his childhood in Wivenhoe and he brings us back to the smell:

"Over all was the acrid smell of guano, disputing for supremacy with the smarting odour given off by a mountain of sprats awaiting farmer's carts and mingled with the effluvium rising from the soft oose of the river".

The decaying sprats were spread on the land as manure and those found in Wivenhoe churchyard mentioned above must have been going off and dumped.

It is a very much earlier Churchwarden's accounts, of 1489 for Walberswick, that we look at next:

"The sed two men to get rekenynge of the heryings and sperlinges". Sperlings or sparlings were sprats. Sparlyng is Old English.

The best smell, of course, that comes from sprats is when they have been floured and crisp fried quickly. There are East Anglians, however, who maintain that the best way to cook sprats is by sprinkling the bottom of the frying pan with salt before putting in the sprats and frying them without fat, letting the salt draw out the fat. When I have tried this method the sprats have been too salt so I will leave the subject with an Essex woman's memory from the early years of our century, "Sometimes on Saturday mother would have sprats put on skewers and cooked in front of the fire". Today kebabs and barbecued sardines are all the rage. Does that leave the Edwardian local housewife ahead of her time or put today's fashionable cookery pundits, who urge us to "eat foreign", *behind* theirs?

SWEETS

Norah Ponder was born in 1907, the daughter of a seed and strawberry grower in Tiptree. I have used her memory to represent that of many other similar ones, "Mrs Hall, known as Ginny, kept the off licence. She used to make peppermint bull's-eyes, orange and lemon drops and coconut ice. You could buy quite a lot for a half penny, which I might add is all we had for a week until we were old enough to earn it". My own memory is of the extraordinary patience of various Essex sweet-shop ladies as they waited for small children whose noses barely reached the counter, clutching their pennies and taking an incredibly long time to choose.

Kate Rose (born 1882, Polstead) also spoke for several other of my older informants, "We used to have sweets by scrambling for them at the treat. They were thrown in the air by the Superintendent of the Sunday school". Others have mentioned the squire, the parson and the schoolmistress as the distributors of this sweetmeat largesse. Earlier in the century nuts are often mentioned as the objects scrambled for.

The children of earlier centuries had a sweet tooth. Jane Taylor, of Colchester, writing about 1800, provides a cautionary tale,

"Do look at those pigs as they lie in the straw,"
Said Dick to his father one day
"They keep eating longer than ever I saw
What nasty fat gluttons are they."
"I see they are feasting," his father reply'd,
"They eat a great deal I allow
But let us remember, before we deride
Tis the nature, my dear, of a sow.
But if a great boy for ever takes picks
At sweetmeats and comfits and figs
Pray let him get rid of his own nasty tricks
And then he may laugh at the pigs."

Comfits were candied fruits or roots. An Essex Still Room book of the 18th century gives the way to make Muskedyne Cumfits. These were raisins. A root much used was that of Eryngo known as Sea Holly which grows on the coast and has large, fleshy and brittle roots which extend for a great distance into the sand. When candied, pieces of these roots were known as kissing comfits. A 17th century Colchester apothecary made great quantities of them and sent them all over England. In the 18th century they were exported from a Colchester manufactory to many parts of the British Empire. The Stuarts believed that eating them kept adults youthful. The kissing in the title seems to suggest that they also kept you lusty.

Eryngo root is mentioned in recipes for 1609 and 1654 ('A True Gentlewoman's Delight') and, in the 17th century, was used in seed cake, rather as today's cake makers use candied peel.

Boiled sweets were made on a commercial scale in Thaxted for over a hundred years by George Lee & Co. My paternal grandfather had a shop in Wivenhoe and sold a lot of them from their attractive glass jars arranged along a shelf. Lee's Alpine Mints were his favourites.

Cleanliness at Thaxted was taken very seriously. I am not so sure that it was by some of the cottage sweet makers. The latter were often to be found strategically placed near village schools. In one Essex village that I lived in, several older inhabitants reminisced to me about their local sweet maker's products which, whatever their colour or type, had the same grey, dirty coloured stripes in them. As they grew up they began to have suspicions about what the grey streaks were.

Moor tells that in the early 18th century "Rock or Rock of Gibraltar was cakes of inspissated treacle streaked somewhat curiously with tight lines of flour, and sold under these names in Suffolk."

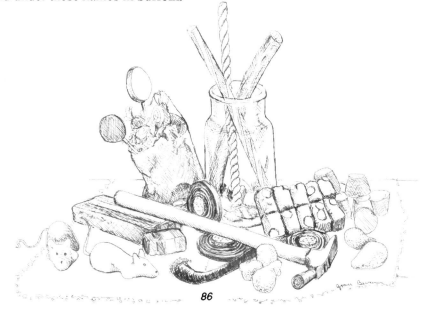

VEGETARIANS

Many of our forebears had vegetarian meals more because they couldn't afford meat rather than have an objection to it. Most vegetables have been treated separately already in this book so this section is devoted to one or two made-up dishes.

SUFFOLK VEGETABLE PIE   First boil some cubed turnips, carrots and onions till tender. To make the crust mix flour, baking powder, herbs and salt and rub in some fat. Having cooked some potato, mash it and lightly mix it in. Add a little grated cheese and mix to a dryish dough by adding a little water. You then roll it out and put it on top of the vegetables in a dish and bake it.

Celeriac, fennel, sweet potato and many other more exotic vegetables are available in the shops today. They can be added to the sort of vegetable pie above. There is no need to buy commercially made vegetable stocks. Onions or leeks (perhaps with some tomatoes) can be reduced down and a little yeast extract will intensify them.

VEGETARIAN DIET, CHEESE PUDDING   4 tablespoons bread crumbs and 2 of grated cheese, 1/2 pint of milk and same of water, 1 egg, 1/2 teaspoon of mustard. Warm the milk and pour over the bread crumbs, add cheese and the egg which has been well beaten, the mustard and salt. Pour it into a pie dish and bake for 20 minutes.

Baked celery custard is another Suffolk dish.

CARROT PUDDING (Essex 17th Century)   To the crum of a 2 penny loaf (and grate it) and half as much grated carrot, and 6 eggs, put 4 whites and some sugar and half a nutmeg, a little salt; mix it with a pint and a pint and a half of cream and you must put into the oven; melt a quarter of a pound or better of fresh butter, put a little rose water, 2 or 3 spoonfuls of sack, then put it into the oven in a dish and let it stand half an hour; the oven must not be too hot.

This is too rich for puritanical vegetarians. I have not attempted it therefore – but I thought you might like to work out from this not entirely clear account how to make it.

VEAL

Essex people were called Essex Calves and John Ray of Black Notley said, in the 17th century, that the expression had its origin in Essex producing "the fattest, fairest and finest flesh in England". Not only did the region have very good grazing near the coast and along the rivers but it also had London nearby as a market for its meat. Ray added that Essex butchers became rich and were buried with monuments suitable for much prouder men. John Morley who had a butcher's shop in Halstead certainly became rich and was obsessed with leaving memorials of himself, but his wealth came from speculation and land jobbery.

George Theodore Manning of Sible Hedingham wrote his 'Rural Rhymes' in the early Victorian period and proclaimed:

Essex, you say, is famed for Calves.
We thank you really for your pains
For thus you prove in our behalves
We're famous most for Head and Brains

Calves' heads were cut in half, soaked, washed and boiled; then served with a parsley and brain sauce. However, although Essex men were called calves, they did not eat very much veal. There was good grazing to turn it into beef and they tended to leave veal to the French. It is sometimes found with other ingredients in various mixtures, nevertheless. An 18th century recipe for sausages contains minced veal together with an equal quantity of beef suet and flavoured with sage and spices. A Sudbury M.S, recipe book has:

VEAL CAKE   Mix equal quantities of minced veal and cooked rice with an egg beaten in milk. Add flavouring, put in a greased mould and steam .

Calves foot jelly is mentioned in the invalids' section so that brings us to R.S.V.P. No, this is not a request to the reader to write in with comments and additions (though these will be welcome) but it was a Suffolk abbreviation for Rump Steak and Veal Pie. Rather succulent and very promising that may sound; but, in our household we haven't touched veal for years after the alarming accounts of the way some veal calves were reared and kept, so there has been a principled but rather reluctant decision not to try R.S.V.P. for this book.

Thomas Nashe writing in Elizabethan times told the story of four hungry fellows in four separate rooms for a year and a day and fed on beef, pork, mutton or veal. The last, the Essex calf , shuddered, quaked and limped, with a visage pale and lamentably vociferated, Veal, Veal, Veal. Nashe then added, " . . . he that ties himself to eat Herring shall beget a child that will be a commander before he hath cast his first teeth". So much for veal!

VERJUICE

During the 16th and 17th centuries much use was made of verjuice. It was the juice of bitter or unripe fruit, normally crab apples. The juice of citrus fruits has taken its place today. The 16th century East Anglian writer, Thomas Tusser, of whom it was said that "he spread his bread with all sorts of butter but none of it would stick thereon" mentions verjuice and says it was a useful winter pick-me-up for ailing cattle as well as for its culinary uses.

October's Husbandrie
Be sure of vergis (a gallond at least)
So good for the kitchen, so needfull for beast,
It helpeth thy cattel so feeble and faint
If timely such cattel with it thou acquaint.

A writer of 1710 ticks people off for paying a great "price for lemons and limes from abroad and despising the crab". Sauces for meat, fish and pies used verjuice together with butter and egg yolks. In 17th century recipes verjuice or vergis was used when boiling capon, mallard, teal or "wigin". Sparrows and larkes were boiled in mutton broth to which mace, herbs and the pressed juice were added. Just as today lemon juice is used with fish so in previous times verjuice was used when "boyling a Flaunder or Pickerel" (flounder or pike). Again herbs and mace were in the broth together with wine, butter and seasoning – top table fare, of course. The Norfolk writer L. Rider Haggard quotes the Book of Knowledge of 1750 on verjuice and Tusser said Michaelmas was the time to make it as the year declined.

Knowing what excellently flavoured jellies are made from very acid fruits like crab apples and sloes, I can believe that verjuice was a great improver of fish and meat. I have many times discovered that it is very unwise to proclaim that a dialect word has died out so I will not state that verjuice finished long ago; but I have never heard it mentioned by any of my East Anglian or Essex informants, even those with memories of grandmothers' ways with food.

Wine and Home Brewed

WINE AND HOME BREWED

William Harrison of Radwinter wrote in 1587, "There is a kind of swish-swash made in Essex with honeycombs and water, which the homely country wives putting some pepper and a little other spice among, call mead – very good in mine opinion for such as love to be loose-bodied at large or a little eased of the cough – otherwise it differeth so much from the true metheglin (mead) as chalk from cheese. Truly it is nothing else but the washing of the combs when the honey is wrung out, and one of the best things that I know belonging therto is that they spend but little labour and less cost in making the same and therefore no great loss if it were never occupied".

A story from Shalford by Walter Harvey (b.1893) suggests that Essex men did not always get their due meed. A beekeeper in an adjoining village lost two hives of honey. The local constable called on two men of Shalford and found them both making mead in the wash house, but no case was made of the incident.

A Wivenhoe WEA student provided me with a bottle of home brewed made with honey in 1988 so that I could have my own horkey (q.v.) This was so good that I am sure it was not made from comb washings.

Bottles, stone jars and other receptacles feature largely in paintings and photographs of the men at work in the countryside. Home brewed beer or cold tea were the usual contents of them in the later years. One Essex man told me that he was nearly converted to cold tea by a threshing engine driver who was a London man. "Nearly" you'll note.

"My father brewed his beer so did my neighbour – that had a lovely twang to it," said Kathleen Chapman of Finchingfield. Home brewing has come back with a bang if not a twang. Earlier in this century the farmers still provided brewing apparatus on the farm premises for their men to brew their own.

A Suffolk 90-year-old made clear the importance of having your own country wine on hand to offer visitors, "Father made lovely Rhubarb wine. Relatives who came from London to visit Granny always came to our house for Uncle John's Rhubarb". Dolly Argent of Great Maplestead said that a drop of home made wine was taken for most ills and that great quantities of it were drunk. Her Uncle Frank used to buy a whole case of oranges when he was making his. A lot of rhubarb and parsnip was made because the basic ingredients were reasonably easy to get hold of.

Celery wine was a favourite in Suffolk and Gooseberry in Essex. Indeed Essex seems to have liked gooseberries generally. I tasted a very good Gooseberry made by a Shalford resident in 1985. It was dry and had an excellent flavour. The Mulberry wine at Stebbing was also excellent.

My recipe comes from a family recipe book from Coggeshall. Elder wine was often drunk with Kitchels (q.v.) on New Year's Eve.

ELDER WINE Put 2 quarts of berries to 4 quarts of water. Let them boil one hour, then strain them, put the strained liquor into the copper again and put 3³/₄ lb of very good sugar to every gallon of liquor. Let them boil one hour, then strain them, put the strained liquor into the copper again and put 3³/₄ lb of good sugar to every gallon of liquor. Add 2 oz of cloves, ¹/₄ lb of ginger, 2 oz of allspice to the 9 gallons. Let it boil an hour, strain off the spice and when of a proper coolness, that is about lukewarm, have a round of bread cut rather thin and toast it, then wet it on both sides with good yeast and put it into the middle of the tub. Cover it over and let it stand two days (Mind it works) then put it into the cask. When it has done working put a new laid egg well beaten and a pound of raisins. Then bung it up. At Christmas put 1 oz of bruised cloves into it but do not stir it. This is 9 gallons. I remember the berries had to be picked from the stalks. Some put a bottle of brandy but I do not. (This is very good wine)

Modern wine makers don't use "coppers, tubs and casks" but I thought you would enjoy the recipe. Recipes for Paigle wine have been handed down for centuries in East Anglia. The pronunciation varied: paigle, peggles and paggles. If I tell you that a man with jaundice was said to be as yellow as a paigle then foreigners may guess that they call paigles cowslips. A Suffolk writer of 1820 has the following, "Six pounds of blows (blossoms) to ten gallons of water is the receipt for paigle wine". The quantities in the Coggeshall and Suffolk recipes seem to bear out suggestions that enormous quantities of country wines were made and consumed by our forebears. I once talked to an Essex wine makers group and the number of bottles they brought along for sampling led me to believe that today's makers don't do too badly. One member said I should try some of his friend's special. His friend was a barber and the chief ingredient was said to be hair clippings.

HOME BREWED BEER

Readers, having mentioned yeast and beer I will now write of the making of home-brewed beer. Teetotallers crack up tea, coffee, cocoa or minerals – I say let them drink them by all means but why find so much fault with beer, when many say they have never tasted it. I do not believe they would have complained had they some of it in their mother's milk, if their mothers had suckled them. If it were good home-brewed beer made from hops and malt, with not too much water with it in the making; neither begrudging it wasting when boiling if they had the average amount to fill up. This was two half-hogshead casks (i) with a few gallons over to be put in bottles of one or two gallons to drink before the casks were ready to broach. Which would be after it had done working say eight or nine days. Then the bung could be put in the casks ready to put the tap in when the bottles were empty.

Well to brew a sack of malt and 5 lb of hops need a bit of doing, for it cannot be well done in a day. For one has to get water, yes from a long way some times. Around our district the majority of men that worked on the farms brewed just before harvest. Farmers would lend a man a horse and water cart to get water from a good pond or spring for the occasion, although very few times did we need that. Then there was the wood to cut. Large round wood generally with a little coal is best. For with coal and wood together the water or beer in the copper can soon be got to boil. Then a slow fire. after.

The copper is first filled with water, providing all the tubs and the mash tun is ready for use (ii), for I know after a spell of hot and dry weather everything leaks that is of wood. So these have to be stenched – wetted from time to time to get the staves of the tubs to swell close so they will hold liquid. It takes quite a time for them to do so at times unless they can be put in a pond, etc.

First the water is boiled, then put in the mash tun with cold water added until scalding hot, for the fine malt must not dumple up or it cannot be wetted. The malt is let slowly into the tun one stirring all the time.

If there is not quite enough water more boiling water is added from the copper. This is the first wort. It is stirred well and then covered up for four hours or a little less to get it ready for the second wort. The first is drawn out to a low tub generally called an under bank (iii). That will not hold all, so a wort tub is brought out to hold the surplus. Enough water is then taken out of the copper for the second wort.

The first wort is then put into the copper quickly so that the copper does not burn. The second wort is stirred well and covered up for the four hours whilst the first wort is being boiled. Hops were put into the copper as soon as there was enough wort in the copper to wet them (iv). All the first wort was put into the copper to boil till the four hours were up and when the second was ready to come off.

This first wort is called Sweet Wort, nice to drink a little of, being very sweet. It is also good to make vinegar – the very best, although we never made it. When the first beer is taken out it is put through a wicker basket called a strainer. Yes beer will not go through after this has been used for some years, it then has to be knocked for the beer to go through. It often makes me think of a man who once brewed at some neighbour of his. He found that everything in the way of tubs and mash tun leaked. He told someone that "everything runned except the strainer". And I know that is a job to get beer through after being used a number of times.

After the two worts are made into beer this is put into two tubs for working. When it is cool enough, for it will not work if too hot or too cold – luke warm is best – yeast is added and stirred well in. Soon if it is working there is a good crop of yeast on the two tubs. Then after a day this new yeast is taken off and the beer put into the casks to be used when needed. It is not long before the tap can be put in. If the malt and hops are good then this is good to drink as soon as it has settled down again.

It is quite fit to drink. Yes good too to take in the fields where one cannot get home to dinner. Nothing better, and I know if one has very hard work to do if he drinks a pint of that it is better than tea, coffee or cocoa to work with. And one can drink a good lot before it would muddle any man at any kind of work, if used as beer should be, not drinking for the sake of drinking.

NOTES

(i)   A whole Hogshead cask held over 50 gallons.

(ii)   The cleaning of utensils was very important. These were scrubbed, chained, scalded and boiled if possible.

(iii)   Through the wicker strainer? It is not clear whether this was used here, for if not fresh malt had to be added to the second wort. This would not be normal practice.

(iv)   Probably not all at the same time as it was customary to add a few more hops after the first straining. The second brewing was inevitably weaker beer. First wort gave strong beer. The second wort produced mild or small beer.

Utensil names: (Some Suffolk ones)

1. Keeler – Brewing Tub. Mash Tun.
2. Underdeck – underback – underbank.
3. Beer stool.
4. Horse-hair sieve – wicker strainer used here.
5. Tunnel – Funnel.
6. Rack (tongs) to rest sieve over tub.
7. Handscup or jet – a ladle.
8. Wilch (Wilsh) bottle shaped wicker filter (see 4 above).
9. Wort Tub.

The following extract by Tulip gives another glimpse into the use of wooden containers. I wonder if Kelier is the Essex for Keeler.

If the weather was fine that was when the boys (Tulip's sons) had to go in the hoops as we called it. This was a large bath we had. If not the wash kelier was used. A kelier was a low tub with a wide ashen hoop made for the top to lift it about by and good things too to wash their clothes in. Very few iron baths or tinned things in the early days. Many wooden pails were used for drinking water to be fetched and to stand in. Galvanised pails were not good for water to stand in. Beer that had aged a bit was even worse. Folk were ill if they drank old ale out of these pails.

A note written by Tulip about hops

The hop grows wild in several places in the parish in hedges near springs or wet ditches. These trail a long way about hedges and have some lovely hops on in some seasons. I have picked them to make home-brewed beer, made with malt and hops.

Joseph Arch's Grace

O Heavenly Father, bless us
And keep us all alive,
There's ten of us for dinner,
And food for only five.